Highland Burn

Guardians of Scotland Book 1

By: Victoria Zak

Highland Burn: Guardians of Scotland Book 1
Victoria Zak
Copyright 2014 by Victoria Zak

Cover Design by JAB Designs

Editing by Julie Roberts

ISBN-13: 978-1500606930
ISBN-10: 1500606936

Contents

Acknowledgments

When I set out to pursue writing my first novel, I knew it had to have a few key elements in order for me to stay focused and entertained. I wanted to write what I was passionate about... dragons. And the next element had to be romance. I knew from the beginning that I wanted to write a romance novel, that was a given. And I knew what I didn't want... a vanilla romance with no exciting toppings.

I wanted a Rocky Road romance covered in sweetness. A story line that had an interesting flavor leaving your taste buds wanting more. A hero and heroine who added that special secret ingredient... magic. And secondary characters who would sparkle, topping my story with sprinkles.

When the first scene hit me, of course I was mopping my floors at the time, and stopping to take notes seemed like a great excuse. Well, a man and woman at a loch came into view. They were destined to be together, but didn't know it yet. Wait? What? A loch? Then mountains and mist began to appear and a man's voice said, "Lass, what are ye waiting for? I have a story to tell ye." A Highlander? Great, I have a Scottish romance novel to write. But what about my dragons? Being that my main character was a true Highlander, he wasn't keen on the whole dragon shifting abilities and paranormal magic. But after a few bribes, and an extra sex scene, he agreed and off I went to write a Scottish medieval paranormal romance.

Along this roller coaster of a ride they call writing a novel, I couldn't have conquered my dream without the love and support of a few angels. I'm honored to have each and every one of you in my life.

My husband – Thank you for your love and support and the countless times you stayed up late listening to my crazy ideas. I love you more then you could ever know.

My wonderful and beautiful kids – Thank you guys for being patient with mommy. You guys are my heart.

Suzan Tisdale – You're truly my inspiration. Thank you for your support and friendship. And guess what? I wrote that damn story.

DL Roan – Thank you for your support and friendship. How many text messages did I send you?

Josette – Thank you for helping me with edits and smoothing out the rough edges. Hey, where's my dragon drink?

Julie Roberts – You are amazing!! Thank you for all your hard work whipping Highland Burn into shape.

My Elite Alphas – You know who you are. I'm honored that you guys stuck around with me through this incredible journey. I'm forever indebted to you.

Prologue

Before Scotland was Scotland, two powerful societies ruled the region together. Two kingdoms, intertwined and complementary; one could not flourish without the other. One kingdom belonged to the Scots and the other to Dragonkine. The Kine were a powerful and ancient race, borne by the masters of old. They possessed both a dragon and human spirit and could take the form of each. As legend would have it, they were created to provide balance to the world and heal the wounds of the 'pre-history'.

Throughout their rule, Dragonkine had proven their worth far more than any riches or coin. They were masters when it came to the lay of the land. Because of the magic their inner dragons held, they knew where to plant fields so that harvests would flourish. They knew where to build temples, and with their strength they could build sturdy, lasting villages. The Scots depended on the Kine greatly.

Fierce warriors, Dragonkine defended their realm with unstoppable power and merciless strength, yet they were not infallible. Without a mate, their inner dragons were unstable. Only a Dragonkine female possessed the power to calm the beast inside. Kine women were a rare race of their own. Though their bodies did not take possession of a dragon, their beauty was beyond exquisite, it was magical. Beautiful elegant Celtic knotwork patterns marked their flawless skin from the forefinger up beyond the shoulders, stopping just short of the breast. A mated female was even more alluring. Once mated, the markings on their skin would assume the color of their mate's elemental power. The women were valued as Goddesses and were worshiped by all Dragonkine. If it weren't for their female's grace and their ability to calm the beast inside, a warrior's dragon would take over and unleash hell on Earth.

Together the Scots and Dragonkine fought off many Viking attacks and tribal conflicts, and maintained peace between the kingdoms. They ruled together for over a hundred peaceful years until a sacred bond was broken. Since the time before time, it was forbidden for a human to mate with Dragonkine.

Trouble began when both kings' heirs became of age and were pressured into finding the proper mate.

King Drest, the Dragonkine king, had a beautiful daughter, Vayla Blue. Being that she was of marrying age, her beauty had attracted many strong and wealthy Kine suitors. Not only was the princess appealing, Vayla had the grace of a queen and a loving heart. She was adored by all of her people, but most of all, she was the sparkle in her father's eye.

King Drest loved his daughter more than life itself. Being as she was his only heir to the throne and to carry on his lineage, he protected Vayla and kept her safe, mayhap a little too much. Five elite warriors, who seemed to never leave her side, followed her wherever she went. And when she wasn't being followed, her mother relentlessly dictated to her as to how a proper princess should act and taught her well, for Kine women were the backbone of their society.

One summer morning King Drest called a royal meeting and by midday his great hall was filled with top ranked warriors from both realms including King MacAlpin, the king of the human realm. Urgent business regarding a neighboring tribe crossing borders and pillaging its villages was the discussion at hand.

"Mac, are we to wait for yer son to show up or do we start without him?" King Drest was starting to become impatient with the young lad. Mac should teach his son some manners when it came to being on time.

MacAlpin ran his hand repeatedly down his plaited beard as he stood by the window sternly eyeing his son hastily making his way through the bailey, winking an eye as he passed by a group of Dragonkine females. "He'll be here," he grumbled.

Constantine, King MacAlpin's son and heir to the throne, charmed the ladies with his vivid green eyes, chiseled jaw, and long sandy blonde hair with war braids framing his boyish face. As beautiful as he was, the Gods had blessed him with brawn and brains, yet his maturity was still questionable.

MacAlpin glared at Constantine as he entered the great hall. He loved his son, but the boy needed discipline. Not that he wasn't honorable or respectful, but trouble just seemed to find him. MacAlpin blamed his wife for allowing Constantine to run amuck, for he could do no wrong in her eyes.

Once everyone was seated, King Drest called the first order of business. Constantine became bored with the mundane arguing and found himself looking out of a window daydreaming, when a beautiful woman came into view. Her long tawny hair streamed down her back in parted waves enticing his eyes to feast upon her. A white gown outlined in gold hugged her body, revealing her slender figure and full round breasts. His head perked up when bright blue eyes caught his stare. Constantine was too busy admiring her curves to notice a small green dragon perched on her shoulder. She was feeding him some kind of fruit.

Constantine thought he would never take another breath when she flashed him an irresistible smile. He knew right then and there that this woman, nay this magnificent woman, had to be his wife. He wouldn't settle for less.

The meeting took forever; at least for Constantine it did. He couldn't wait to track his woman down and it didn't help that he was as hard as a rock. He kept shifting in his seat trying to relieve the stiffness. He even tried thinking about their hag of a cook back home, naked, but nothing was going to satisfy his need until he claimed his obsession.

Once the meeting was over he found her. She playfully led him back behind a rowan tree where they tore off each other's clothing, their hands exploring each other as he kissed her like no other, soft and slow, building up to an unquenchable rapture. Vayla surrendered to her own needs as Constantine backed her up against the tree and claimed her ever so sweetly.

As lust was finally sated, Constantine laid her down upon lush green grass and made love to her again, but this time he took his time discovering her luscious body. He couldn't get enough of her soft skin, womanly curves, and her long lean legs.

After they had their fill of each other, Constantine fell asleep with his head on Vayla's lap. As she watched Constantine sleep, she made a small cross out of twigs from the rowan tree and bound the sticks together with strands of her golden hair. This was forbidden. Dragonkine women were never to marry or bed a human. They both knew that, yet their hearts knew no boundaries.

Before Constantine left, she placed the cross in his hands. "May this protect ye until we meet again." It was as though she knew what the outcome of this beautiful rebellion was going to be. He kissed her and headed back to his home. It would be the last time he saw her.

Chapter 1

The Loch
Late summer of 1314
Medieval Scotland

"Fergus, the water is verra refreshing. Why don't ye join me?"

The white stallion inhaled deeply then snorted, as he ate from a patch of lush green grass.

"Well, ye dinnae have to be rude about it."

Long white hair with streaks of gray fell over his muscled neck as the fine steed shook his head and stomped his hoof. He pulled on a blade of grass, indicating that he was perfectly content grazing near the loch's edge.

A slight giggle escaped her mouth as she splashed at her horse.

Abigale Bruce had ridden hard and fast through the glen most of the morn. Since her father's recent successful victory over the English at the battle of Bannockburn, Abigale had been freed from the nunnery. Her excitement of finally being able to explore her new-found freedom was too much to hold back as she charged through the forest. Now she rewarded Fergus with a patch of grass while she cooled off in the loch. Oh how she cherished these moments; they were few and far between.

Eight long years at Dunfermline Abbey wasn't the ideal place to grow up, but she had no choice in the matter. Her father, Robert the Bruce, King of Scotland, had placed her there in order to keep her safe from his enemy, the English. Throughout her time at the Abbey, King Edward, the King of England, had gotten close to capturing her a few times, but the small secretive community of nuns had held true to their oath and kept her hidden well.

Unhappy about the newly crowned King of Scotland, the English had captured Abigale's step-mother, half-sister, and her two aunts, and had also beheaded three of her uncles. Humiliated, held prisoner behind iron bars of a bird cage, and hung from the Tower of London had been the women's fate. Even though her freedom was taken away, Abigale knew it was nothing compared to what they had endured.

Abigale's trouble had started as soon as she walked through the gates of the abbey. Robert Bruce had given Dunfermline Abbey a generous contribution to repair part of the church that had been attacked by King Edward. In return he requested that Abbot Benard take his daughter in and protect her. With such a gracious amount of coin given, the Abbot could not refuse. Therefore Abigale, at the wee age of ten, had been left at the abbey and placed in the cruel hands of Abbess Margaret.

Since Abbess Margaret was in charge of twelve nuns, she declared she had not the time to look after the wee brat, so she left Sister Kate in charge of Abigale. Abbess Margaret was a beautiful middle-aged woman with short, raven hair, and possessed the ability to inflict the cruelest of punishments. She watched and waited for Abigale to slip up so she could take pleasure in punishing her. Abigale knew why the woman hated her; she was jealous and thought it unfair that she had special treatment just because she was the king's daughter.

Abigale was afforded a few exceptions to the rules. Because of her lack of interest in taking the vow to become a nun, she didn't have to cut her hair like the other sisters. Furthermore, she could marry, and own property. Although there was one rule that had to be followed; she had to be obedient. And Abbess Margaret took great pride in punishing a disobedient Abigale. Sending Abigale on a daily pee pot cleaning always seemed to make the corners of her thin lips twitch. "Ye're no princess, a bastart child who her own father has abandoned."

After a few missed visits from her father and daily tongue lashings from Abbess Margaret, Abigale started to feel pushed aside and abandoned, yet her spirit held firm.

Sister Kate had kept a watchful eye on Abigale, keeping her workload full so she would stay out of trouble, but trouble seemed to follow her wherever she went as if she was born into it. Abbey life wasn't the life for her. She grew to hate the prayer bells, for they rang eight times during the day starting at the wee hours of night. The blasted bell would ring either when she was sound asleep or assisting a monk in surgery. More times than not she was late to prayer and being tardy was frowned upon. The consequences were harsh, in fact they were harsher than falling asleep during worship. Abigale knew this all too well; she had fallen asleep in a choir stall one night. Sister Kate had been the circator that night, pacing up and down the aisle as she shined her bright cresset lamp into the stalls checking if anyone had fallen asleep. A sharp point with a stick to her ribcage had woken Abigale up quickly. Of course she got a rap on the legs for that one. Thank God it was Sister Kate, for she showed her mercy.

Now that she was home, her father was more than ever adamant about keeping his family safe. He vowed to never allow another Bruce woman to be captured by the filthy Sassenach. Just as Abigale thought she'd regained her freedom, here she was once again with it ripped away from her by an arranged marriage to her father's first in command. Who better to protect her than the Bogeyman himself?

Trepidation crept over her, sending a shiver through her body as she thought about the man her father had arranged for her betrothal. *"The Black Douglas,"* she thought. A man with a reputation that would make the Devil himself shudder with fear. A ruthless warrior who had fought in many battles with her father. The English feared him terribly, making up nursery rhymes warning their wee bairns to *"hush before the Black Douglas will get ye".* She'd never met the man before, but the deal was done. Her father had arranged the marriage and Abigale was to abide by his orders.

Abigale turned to Fergus who was chewing on a blade of grass. "At least ye don't have to marry the Bogeyman." She shuddered. Saying it out loud made it all too real.

For a moment she wondered just what the Black Douglas would look like. Could her father be so cruel as to wed her to an evil, battle-worn old man? Nay, who could possibly be scared of an old man? Then again, a warrior's reputation lived on even after death. Or mayhap he really was a monster of some sort, a mythical creature of the night that lurked under your bed waiting to nip at your heels. Abigale was letting her imagination get the best of her. Shaking those thoughts from her head she dipped down into the coolness of the loch, washing away every bit of worry. Today was her day and she was going to enjoy the peace that the loch gave her before it was taken away from her.

Coming back up she lay her body out flat to float on top of the water's surface. Her light linen shift clung to her petite body, long dark auburn hair spread out and floated with the ripples of the water. Closing her eyes, she opened her arms out wide allowing her fears to fall from her body and sink to the bottom of the loch.

A snapping of twigs alerted Abigale that she wasn't alone. Quickly she dipped her body down into the water to hide from what was lurking in the woods. Panic pricked up her spine as she searched the glen's wooded edge for some kind of movement. Nothing... no movement at all. It must be a small animal frolicking through the thicket. Another snap. This time it sounded too close and too loud to be a small animal.

Abigale turned and faced Fergus.

Ears pointing in the direction of the snapping sound, Fergus let out a gut deep neigh.

"Ye heard that too?" she whispered, trying not to draw attention to herself. Abigale slowly moved toward the water's edge, not making a sound. The last thing she needed was to be attacked by a wild animal or worst yet... a rogue Highlander.

Dripping wet and cold, Abigale stepped out of the water and headed straight for the huge boulder covered in green moss where her dress and her dirk lay. If instincts had taught her anything, it was to never let your guard down and never leave home without your dirk.

A third snap sounded like it came from behind her and way too close. Taking a steady breath, she grabbed her dirk and spun around to meet her attacker face to face. Lunging the blade forward she pointed it at his throat, the tip inches away from piercing it.

"Och lass, I will no hurt ye." A massive six-foot-four man with vibrant amber eyes stood before her with his hands up in surrender.

Abigale arched a dark brow over deep blue eyes. "How do I know I can trust ye?"

"I have no weapons on me… frisk me if ye dinnae believe me." With a sly grin he turned around with his arms in the air inviting her eyes to gaze upon every inch of his muscular body.

Abigale took him up on his offer, for she could not will her eyes off him if she tried. Following his every move, her body came alive. Her hands began to itch as she thought about running them down the corded muscles that lined his abdomen. Hulking arms shimmered in the sunrays as if they had been kissed by the sun and she wondered how his arms would feel wrapped around her body. As he turned around, long black hair hung over his big broad shoulders and stopped at his shoulder blades. His lower back tapered in to a firm backside which was covered in a black and gray plaid. Funny… she had a sudden urge to squeeze his buttocks. God could not have forged a more perfect man, she thought.

Being ten-and-eight, innocent, and sheltered behind the walls of the nunnery, she hadn't had much of a chance to explore the ways of men. In fact if she wasn't praying, she was in the infirmary mending men severely wounded from battle, or ill. Sister Kate's nagging voice reminded her that "Ye only have room for one man in yer heart and He would never steer ye wrong." Only if Sister Kate could see this man standing before her now, even she would blush.

"Ye should no be sneaking up on me like that." Abigale lowered the dirk, but still kept her grip tight.

The alluring man crossed his massive arms in front of his bare chest. "I was taking a rest while out riding when I saw ye over here. Ye know a bonny young lass like yerself should no be oot alone without an escort."

"I can take care of myself just fine."

"Aye, I can see that." He rubbed his throat.

She stood shivering from the cold or mayhap from the intensity of his gaze; she needed to retrieve her clothes before she caught her death. Then she remembered that she was wearing a thin shift. Surely he could see right through to her naked body? Quickly with her free hand she tried to cover her breasts and still have some dignity. "Would ye kindly turn around now so I can dress?" She motioned with the dirk for him to turn around.

He turned, giving her privacy to dress. "That's a fine horse ye have there," he said over his shoulder.

Abigale finished dressing and began to smooth the wrinkles out from her dress with her hands. "That's Fergus, he's a gift from my da. A true warhorse."

Of the few times her father had come to visit her at the abbey, and there were only a few, she remembered the day when he had brought Fergus to her as a gift. A gift perhaps but more like a peace offering for being absent for over a year. Abigale forgave her father, and the white charger quickly became more than a horse, he was a friend.

"Ye may turn around now." As Abigale glanced up, her heart skipped a beat as amber eyes pierced her, sending a rush of heat through her body. She licked her lips and struggled to swallow past a dry throat. How could this man, who she had never met before, make her hunger for something that she had not yet had? Feeling uneasy, she broke their stare and quickly searched for her shoes.

"Are ye a Highlander?" What kind of a question was that? Of course he was a Highlander… that was a plaid he wore. *Way to go, Abigale Bruce, he must think I'm a real dunderhead.*

"Why do ye ask?"

"That is a plaid ye wear?" Abigale leaned against the boulder and bent down to slip on her shoes.

"Aye."

"Then ye must be a Highlander."

Indeed the ways of Highlanders were much different from the English-influenced ways of lowland men like her father. Still both parties had fought for Scotland until the crown and riches were in their grasp. Some would say that greed was the root of all evil. Abigale thought differently. The crown was the root of all evil. Men fought for it, killed for it, and sold their souls for a taste of the crown and the power it held. The crown grew evil in men and she knew that all too well because it was her father's own greed for the crown that left her abandoned at the abbey.

The unsettled nature of Scotland had left Abigale hardened. She'd seen firsthand the aftermath of battles fought; mended wounds, prayed over dead bodies, and even buried the dead. The nunnery where she grew up would set up tents to aid those wounded in battle. Abigale would assist in surgery and her passion grew for healing the sick and mending wounds. Life was to be valued, not destroyed.

In a way she blamed Lady Scotland for her misfortunes. Her father's growing need to fight for Scotland had caused her to stay hidden, conceal her true identity, and grow up without a family. Her whole family had been affected by the battles fought for Scotland and the greed of claiming the crown. Though it was true she had long forgiven the Lady; she could not forget.

The Highlander seemed far away in thought, because he took a while to answer. "Some would say I'm a Highlander." He approached Abigale. "May I?" The beautiful stranger reached for a piece of hair that was stuck to her face and tucked it behind her ear. He brushed a callused finger down her cheek to her slender neck leaving a fiery path trailing behind.

He held her stare and captivated her to the point that she could not form a coherent thought. Her body was no longer hers to control, her heart dropped, and desire pooled in her core setting her body on fire. This Highlander was so close to her she could feel his breath on her skin, she could smell his masculine scent and soon she wanted to taste his lips.

The mysterious man lowered his head, cupped his hand behind her neck, and pulled her close to him to claim her lips. Abigale drew in a deep breath in anticipation when suddenly a nudge from behind broke her trance. She turned to find Fergus.

"Fergus!" she scolded. "What's gotten into ye?"

Another nudge by a wet gray muzzle almost sent Abigale to the ground until strong arms caught her around the waist. "I got ye lass," he whispered in her ear.

For some odd reason the deep rich tone of his voice soothed her. She closed her eyes, took a deep breath and leaned back against the warmth of his body. Wait… what was she doing? *Abigale Bruce, you are to be married.*

Quickly she slipped away from his hold and began to gather up the leather reins. "I should be getting back." Observing the stallion's actions, it was clear to Abigale that Fergus did not approve of the stranger.

Jumping up on the back of Fergus, she turned to face the Highlander. The man rubbed the back of his neck as if he was thanking the white horse for saving his arse from making a huge mistake.

She dared one last look at him before she rode off into the glen back to her father's castle where she would prepare for travel to Castle Douglas and marry the Bogeyman. Her eyes roamed his massive body sketching everything about him to memory; his striking amber eyes, strong masculine jaw line, and the way his eyes strayed over her body. She did not want to forget this man.

If only she did not have to go. Mayhap she could run away with this beautiful man and avoid being married to a monster. Deep down, she was drawn to this mysteriously intriguing, charming and pure male Highlander. He made her think that for once she could be in control of her life and make her own decisions. In a way she envied his freedom. It did not seem fair that she had to marry a man who her father wanted her to marry. *Shouldnae one marry for love?* But then again, he was a stranger… a mystery. Before she ran away with fantasies she knew better than to think of, she squeezed her legs, sending Fergus into a run. She had to marry the Bogeyman.

Chapter 2

The Bogeyman

Hush ye, hush ye, little pet ye,
Hush ye, hush ye, do not fret ye,
The Black Douglas shall not get ye.

A thunderous knock echoed through James's bedchamber, and rattled his drunken slumber. He growled his response while rolling over on his back. A soft, warm, naked body nuzzled next to him, sighing a breathy moan.

As his way of dealing with an unwanted arranged marriage, he had spent the night drinking heavily. To his dismay, no amount of mead was going to change his situation. The thought alone of not being in control of his fate burned him. The more he burned the more he drank until he was numb, which meant a significant amount, being that he was Dragonkine.

When a busty brunette with a low-cut dress whispered an invitation of a night filled with pleasures to him, he couldn't resist. It wasn't unusual for women to offer themselves to him. He was handsome, dominating, and a Highlander. Men feared him, and woman sought to have him between their legs. Being the clan chief did have its advantages.

Another loud rap ricocheted through his head. "Go away!" he demanded. "Leave me be."

James drifted back to sleep, when all of a sudden the door flew open with such force it shattered its' hinges. Terrified out of her wits, the brunette sat up and threw her hands over her breasts. As she tried to cover herself, a tall, robust man came charging into the room.

"Conall?" With his vision blurred and head pounding, James could barely recognize his best friend and second in command.

Conall scooped up the brunette's dress and threw it at her. "Get out!"

The frightened woman jumped out of bed naked, and holding her dress, she ran out of the room.

"James get yer arse out of bed," Conall demanded and threw a white tunic at him.

James moaned and tried to sit up; his stomach lurched and his head spun.

"Do ye realize what today is?"

"Aye," James rumbled.

"I'm going now to fetch yer lass. Ye best get moving."

Lass... Lass... James lay there for a moment trying to shake the cobwebs free. "Shite." He scrubbed a hand down his face. Today was the day he was to marry the princess of Scotland.

Before James finished putting on his tunic, a pair of trews smacked him in the face. Conall showed him no mercy. With his hands on his hips he stood looking over at James sternly. "Make sure ye wash up. Ye stink like a dung heap." Conall turned and exited the chamber.

James sat up and did a quick sniff under his armpits. "Aye." His face furrowed.

After his chambermaid prepared his bath, James bathed the mead and wench filth off him. So here he sat at the edge of the bed pulling on his boots, preparing himself to marry a lass from a nunnery who just happened to be the king's daughter. His mood turned dark and vile when he thought of the current situation he was in. What was King Robert thinking when he arranged for his daughter to marry him? Robert knew he was Dragonkine. Slaughtering the enemy on the battlefield was where he belonged, not tied to a lass.

He was a beast... a dragon. Even though born human, he still had gone through one hell of a transformation eighteen years ago at the wee age of ten. Now, he was twenty-and-eight with a fully transformed beast inside.

When his dragon seized control he was uncontainable, a ruthless being wreaking mayhem upon his enemies and leaving a trail of destruction behind. Stealthy raids and ambushes aided him in keeping his dragon a secret. Only attack at night and leave no prisoners behind... kill them all.

There was nothing like it in the world when he shifted. The freedom he felt when he took to the skies was indescribable. Nose to the wind, his senses were strong... slicing through the clouds, his powerful wings dominated... the call of the wild, his blood pulsed with the earth... he was dragon.

Mentally James shook himself and stood. Grumbling a few blasphemies, he grabbed his cloak and flung it over his broad shoulders as he made his way to the door. He knew exactly who he was, which made his situation even more dreadful. He had to come up with a plan to get rid of the princess but still keep his honor. Surely if he made life unbearable for her, she would go running back to her da begging for an annulment. The corners of his mouth began to turn up, along with his mood, as he shut the door and strode off to the kirk.

~~~~~

Abigale gazed at her reflection in the mirror as a chambermaid, Griselda, pulled a comb through Abigale's tangles. She hissed in pain when the comb stumbled upon another knot. "Stop that!" She swatted at the maid.

"Ye ought to be still, lass and stop complaining." Griselda huffed and continued her assault. Apparently Griselda did not care for her much, nor about her wishes. Undoubtedly a miserable person to boot.

"Ye ought to try to be kinder. Ye are yanking my hair out." Abigale picked up a lock of auburn hair from the floor. "Look," she demanded.

This just added to Abigale's foul mood. Her body ached after enduring yesterday's brutal ride to Castle Douglas. Accompanied by four of her father's trusted knights, they stopped in between downpours of cold rain, and rode their horses through the mucky terrain making the ride twice as long as it should have been.

Not to mention the cold welcome she received as they arrived late last night. She found it odd that her husband-to-be was not present to welcome her to her new home. However it pleased her, for she wasn't ready to meet him.

Her stomach rumbled, reminding her that the last thing she had eaten was last night's stale bread and hard cheese that waited for her after her bath. After the long ride her stiff and dirty body had been quite thankful for the bath.

Sleep had evaded her most of the night. Even after a hard day's travel Abigale couldn't escape her fear of meeting the Black Douglas. So many questions invaded her mind. What does the Bogeyman look like and is he real? How would he treat her? Would his breath smell like ale the first time they kissed? But most of all, how would he take her when they consummated their marriage? Would he be rough? She couldn't imagine a man with such a reputation displaying mercy towards an innocent.

Being a laird's wife and raising wee bairns, nay, more like spawns from Satan, was her destiny now. She shuddered at the sheer thought of it. How could her father do this to her? Hadn't she suffered enough by the hands of Abbess Margaret? All she wanted in life was to be happy and have a loving family. Was that too much to ask for?

A plan entered her mind. Mayhap she could run away… find shelter in a small village where no one knew her. Start a life of her own, instead of one that had been arranged.

Just as quickly as hope began to bloom, it withered away. Abigale's forehead creased in defeat. She couldn't live her life on the run. Her father would find her eventually; furthermore, no one escaped the Bogeyman.

A hair-pin pricked her scalp and brought her attention back to the here and now as Griselda shoved it in place. Abigale shrugged out of the way from the rough-handed wench when she saw another pin appear in Griselda's fat hand.

"That will be enough for now." Abigale shooed her away.

Abigale rose on shaky legs and took a step back so she could observe her dress. An off the shoulder white dress hugged her body to perfection. Gold Celtic knots lined the top of her bodice and the bottom of her long sleeves. Her auburn hair sat behind her head, plaited and coiled into a tight bun. Griselda really did do a beautiful job, she thought.

She wished her mother was still alive. Tears filled her eyes as she thought about her mother. A vision flashed of an auburn-haired woman standing in front of her, beaming with pride and holding Abigale in her loving arms. The kind and caring woman would know what to do in times like these.

A loud rap on the door made Abigale flinch, making her situation all too real. Griselda opened the door and informed her that her escort was here to take her to the kirk.

Abigale closed her eyes, trying to fight back the urge to run. To run back to the loch and into the arms of her beautiful Highlander. Mentally, she cursed her father a million times for arranging this nightmare.

"I'll be right there." Walking over to the bed, her hands shook as she picked up a sheer veil with scalloped lace edges. She draped the material over her head, careful not to disturb Griselda's creation, and with one last look in the mirror she squared her shoulders and lifted her chin. Abigale held on to the very last bit of courage she had left. She had survived Abbess Margaret's cruelty, she could surely endure the Black Douglas.

A very tall, well-built man entered the chamber and offered his arm. "My lady."

Abigale accepted, for she had no choice. Tightly she wound her fingers around the escort's arm and they made their way to the kirk.

As Abigale approached the tiny building, she noticed that it looked as if it had been burned. Charred stone marred the outside walls. The remainder of black soot still clouded the stained glass windows and there was the slightest smell of burnt earth in the air.

Fear quickly turned into terror as Abigale reached the wooden double doors of the chapel. Heart racing, hands trembling, she reached for the door then paused. Panic and fear had consumed her as the air became thick, making it hard for her to breathe, and her legs threatened to buckle. She held on to the escort's arm to steady her balance. She clenched her hand to her chest, and began to breathe quickly in and out.

The escort's brows creased. "Are ye ill?"

A muttered nay escaped her lips.

"My lady, look at me." The escort crouched down until he was eye level with Abigale. "Slow… short… breaths…"

Swirling gray-blue eyes that reminded her of raging storm clouds held her stare. Her lungs began to slow to a steady rhythm, and her body felt weightless as if she was under a hypnotic trance.

"Verra good, lass," he reassured her. The escort took pity on her and pushed the door open.

An eerie creaking sound echoed off the stone walls as the door opened. A rush of cold stale air hit her body causing her to shiver and rub her arms warm. The only light that shone through the kirk was a singular sunbeam peering through a small arched window. Abigale watched as dust specks danced in its rays as her eyes adjusted to the darkness. Nay, this is not a place of worship, Abigale thought. 'Tis too cold and dark. But the cloaked figure sitting on the steps next to the pulpit had to be the Black Douglas.

With his hands on the small of her back, the escort nudged her forward. Willing her feet to move and sending a pleading prayer up to the heavens, Abigale stopped in front of the cloaked figure and lowered her head to greet the Black Douglas. "My Laird." Courage... she thought to herself... courage.

The man stood, his wool cloak fell to the ground revealing his face. Abigale's eyes widened in disbelief like she'd seen a ghost. Her mysterious Highlander from the loch stared back at her. A whispered "nay" slipped past her lips. Astonished, she couldn't accept the fact that this man was the same man she had met two days ago.

The Black Douglas dominated the room with his massive frame as he towered over her petite body. His eyes swirled amber like freshly poured whiskey as he intently gazed down at her. His animalistic presence chilled her to the core. A half-moon-shaped scar under his right eye made his blood-chilling stare more sinister. How could she have missed that scar?

"So, ye be the princess of Scotland, aye?" Abigale froze at the sheer roughness of his tone.

He bent down and whispered in her ear. "What's wrong, lass? Afraid of the Bogeyman?"

On the inside Abigale shook with fear, but on the outside she held firm. She caught her breath and nervously let it go before she answered him.

"Nay." Slowly she lifted her veil, tilted her head back, and met his icy stare. "Ye can no be the man from the loch."

It didn't go unnoticed when she saw his brows slightly arch as if he was surprised as well. She must have had some kind of effect on the Bogeyman, because he broke their stare swiftly and began to circle her like an animal hunts its prey.

"And what makes ye think that?"

She swallowed hard to quench her dry throat. "The man at the loch… was a gentleman."

Being this close, she could feel the warmth of his breath sweeping over her skin like a hot summer's night. Her heart pounded so hard that she could feel it drumming against her chest. But what disturbed her the most was the desire heating up deep within her, waking up the flutter of butterflies in her stomach. Aye, this was indeed the same man.

Stopping in front of her, he lifted her chin. The coarseness of his skin reminded her of scales. He arched a black brow and pinned her hard with his amber eyes. "I'm most definitely the same man and I've no claimed to be a gentleman, lass."

Chapter 3

Better to sit all night then to go to bed with a dragon. ~ Zen Proverb

James glanced down at their joined hands. A shaking, tiny hand sat perfectly in his palm as he finished muttering his vows and slipped a ring on Abigale's fourth finger on her left hand. "I receive ye as mine," he repeated and turned back to the priest who stood in front of the pulpit. Frankly, this whole process was taking way too long for James's liking. He clasped his hands in front of him and shifted his weight on his heels. Damn, the priest had a lot to say. A simple "Aye" from both parties would suffice; no need for all these drawn out details.

A blinding glare caught his attention coming from Abigale's left hand. He glanced at her hands, squinting from the sun reflecting off of her wedding band. He cursed silently. Abigale was his wife.

The priest motioned for them to kneel and bow their heads for the blessing. As the ending of the ceremony was closing in on James he realized what came next; consummating the marriage. Sweat began to form on his forehead. He needed to think of something quick, because in no manner was he going to lie with Abigale tonight. Without a doubt he felt her dread in every fiber woven within him; terror had shone through her eyes the moment she entered the kirk. Although his reputation would say differently of him, James was not the monster everyone made him out to be. He would not bed an innocent; not like this.

There was no other way around it, he had to fake the consummation and he had better make it look convincing, for he was going to have to lie to a priest. Since it was customary for the holy one to view the consummation, James had to have a fool-proof plan, but the real problem that lay ahead was convincing Abigale to play along. With her growing up in a nunnery it might not be that easy to persuade her to lie to a priest.

Mayhap he should bed her and be done with it. After all, Abigale's beauty enticed him… beckoned him. Being his wife, she had to know what was expected of her. James pondered this thought a while until his bloody dragon began to pulse through his body reminding him of why he could not bed Abigale. Demons he wished not to speak of ran soul deep, too deep to be forgiven. Abigale deserved better.

"Ye may rise as I announce ye man and wife." With his white robe billowing off his arms, the priest opened them over James and Abigale, embracing their marriage.

James hopped to his feet like his arse was on fire. As soon as Abigale was on her feet, James crouched down in front of her and flung her over his massive shoulder. The plan was in motion.

Tiny hands pounded at his back in protest. "Put me down, James Douglas!" Abigale demanded.

Not listening to a word she was saying, James quit the kirk and made his way to Castle Douglas. As he maneuvered his way through the bailey, Abigale kicked at him, almost causing him to drop her. He slapped a firm, giant hand across her backside. "Enough or I'll drop ye," James warned.

"Ouch!" Abigale squealed and squirmed.

James dodged and weaved through the village; time was of the essence. He had to reach the bedchamber before the priest arrived. If he didn't make it on time then there was no way around it, he would have to bed Abigale in front of the holy one and that could not happen.

Enormous wooden doors opened as James reached the keep of Castle Douglas. His brother, Archibald, stood opening the doors with a confused expression on his face as he looked at James.

"Don't ask." James glanced at his younger brother sternly.

Archibald shook his head and closed the doors behind him.

Walking right past his brother, James continued his way through the great hall until he reached the stairs leading to the second floor. With haste, his long muscled legs took the stairs two at a time until he reached the corridor. Abigale still protesting on his back, he ran down the corridor and slammed into a chambermaid. White linen sheets flew from the chambermaid's hands and littered the floor. The force of the impact turned James's body around and he now faced the maid. "Sorry lass," he said breathing heavily. "Where's the closest unoccupied bedchamber?"

The chambermaid, with a look of surprise on her face, clenched a white sheet to her chest, bowed her head and pointed down the hall. "My Laird, last door to yer left."

There was no time for small talk as he quickly continued to close the distance between him and the nearest bedchamber.

"That-a-lass." The maid called out and shook her head as if she wished it was her being hauled off to a room by a man such as the laird.

Finally, they reached the bedchamber. James shouldered the door open and quickly placed Abigale on her feet, shutting the door behind him.

~~~~~

Abigale stumbled a step back as she gained her balance. Her neatly shaped bun now hung in a ball of tangles. "James Douglas, I demand to know what's going on."

Raking her fingers through her hair, she tried to tame her mass of locks, while her head spun. One moment she was kneeling in front of the priest and then the next she was swept off her feet and carried through the village like a sack of oats. What was going on?

"James?" Abigale harrumphed when he ignored her request.

Without replying, James peeked out of the small window of the chamber's door.

"Who are ye looking for?" Realization hit her like a stone to the head... the priest.

Oh dear God, she had to bed her husband. Even though she knew this day would come it didn't mean she had to like it. Abigale's heart began to race and her palms began to sweat as she started to panic. The man who stood before her was intimidating and intense, but not as vile as she had imagined. Though she couldn't help but feel that he wasn't too fond of her.

What if it hurt? What if she couldn't please him? Worse yet, what if she repulsed him? Every bit of her skin beaded with sweat and her stomach went queasy. Innocent and never being with a man before, Abigale was scared, and completely confused by this man's actions.

Quickly James strode over to Abigale and without saying a word he grabbed her arm and spun her so that her back was facing him. Two large hands grabbed the back of her dress at the neckline and started to rip the material in two. Blessed Mary, he was going to be rough with her. She squeezed her eyes closed, trying to fight back the tears.

A loud rip echoed throughout the bedchamber. On weakened legs, Abigale tried to escape James's grip, but it was of no use, he was too powerful for her to fight. "Stop, please, my Laird," she pleaded. "Please... not like this."

Abigale was swiftly turned around so she had to face him. Her dress barely hung from her shoulders and tears filled her deep blue eyes.

"I dunno how much time we have before the priest arrives." He ripped Abigale's dress off of her and flung it on the floor. She stood naked from the waist up.

Her eyes wide, her body trembling, Abigale's arms immediately flew across her chest trying hard to cover herself.

James tugged his tunic off at the same time he hurried to remove his boots. "Unless ye want to bed me lass, we have to make it look like we've consummated our marriage."

"I dinnae understand." Abigale stood confused. "Are ye telling me we are going to lie and say we've consummated the marriage? Lie to a priest?" This was a mortal sin, lying… to a priest of all people. She would be stripped of grace, condemned to damnation unless she confessed.

"Aye."

Abigale shook her head in disbelief. "'Tis a sin. I can no do it." Was he really asking her to choose between her virginity and faith?

James advanced on Abigale, making her take a step back. "Maybe in your world 'tis a sin but not in mine. I know ye dinnae want to bed me, but the fact is, Abigale, sometime ye must stretch the truth."

Either way she would have to bed her husband, if not tonight then when she confessed her sin. Question still unanswered. *Abigale Bruce what do ye value most your virginity or faith?* Mayhap a little lie now, confess later was her best option right now.

Holding James's amber depths, Abigale, with remorse, tugged the St. Andrew's cross from around her neck and dropped it to the floor. She closed her eyes and prayed for forgiveness as she listened to the ping of the cross hitting the floor.

At that time a loud rap on the chamber's door broke their attention. Their heads snapped toward the door… the priest.

Quickly James bent down in front of her and shoved his hands up her skirts. Callused yet gentle hands slid up her thighs sending an erotic sensation through her body and settling between her legs. Oddly enough, her body began to ache for his touch so much that she almost forgot about the priest. Her hands slowly started to leave her breasts. All she could think about was wanting to plunge her fingers through his hair, and draw him in closer so she could feel his bare skin next to hers. *So, this is lust*, she thought. How quickly he had turned her into a wanton woman.

He unsheathed the dirk strapped to her thigh and dropped her skirt. "Good lass." He smirked.

Before he let her go he bent down and whispered in her ear, "Start moaning."

Confusion swept her face. "What?"

Both of them looked at each other bringing Abigale out of her lustful daze. James nodded, motioning for her to start moaning.

"Oh, my Laird," Abigale moaned uncomfortably but convincing enough.

"Good lass," he whispered with a smile.

All the while Abigale moaned a series of my Lairds, she watched James. With the dirk in one hand he had slit the other until blood dripped to the floor. Racing to the bed he pulled the blankets and furs back until he reached the crisp white linen sheet. Immediately he ripped the sheet from the bed and stained it with his blood. *Perfect evidence*, Abigale thought. He really had thought of everything, for the bloody material looked as if he had in fact penetrated her maidenhood and consummated the marriage. The priest would never know the difference.

As James went forth with his plan, he gestured for her to climb in the bed. Happy to oblige, the moaning ceased and Abigale slipped into bed pulling the covers up to her chin. Somehow being shrouded under the soft furs made her feel protected as if she was invisible. Oh how she wished she could sink further into the blankets.

Peeking over the edge of the fur, her eyes never left James. With the bloodstained sheet in hand, he walked over to answer the door. Before he cracked the hatch he untied his trews and disheveled his hair. This man had thought of everything, Abigale mused. He threw the stained sheet and her ripped wedding dress at the priest then slammed the door.

The priest left as quickly as he came.

James had been right, she did not want to bed him, not after the last couple of days she had been through. Her mind was confused and muddled; one moment she had freedom then the next it was taken away. She had met a beautiful man at the loch only to find out that he was the Bogeyman she was to marry. When James brought her up to the bedchamber she'd thought for sure he would stake his claim, take her roughly, and rob her of everything she held sacred. Men like him took what they wanted and didn't care who they hurt in the process, yet he had showed her mercy. Her nerves threatened to break down and shatter. *Dear Lord, please just make him leave.*

~~~~~

James leaned his back against the door and sighed in relief. The priest was gone, but he still felt like an arse for making Abigale choose between her virginity and her faith. Even though it was her choice, he couldn't shake the feeling; he almost wished he had made the choice for her, to bed the lass and be done with it. After seeing her flawless, peachy skin, her full breasts, and touching her soft thighs, it wouldn't have taken much to change his mind. Like the greedy beast he was he would have taken everything she offered, if she was offering. This is why the lass had to go, he could not be trusted around her and he could feel his self-control slipping away.

As he picked up his tunic from the floor and tugged it on, he paused for a moment and glanced over at the auburn-haired beauty. She looked so innocent with her big deep blue eyes pinning him from over the top of a black fur. God's wounds! She was shaking. He'd frightened her.

As he watched the lass cowering under the fur, his dragon stirred, reminding him he needed to get out of here and fast, for temptation lay right before him, beckoning him. Abigale had encountered enough of the Bogeyman for one night.

With his boots in hand he turned and quit the bedchamber leaving Abigale to rest.

Chapter 4

The dragon teaches you that if you want to climb high you have to do it against the wind. ~ Chinese Proverb

The next morning James busied himself preparing their horses for the long ride back home to Black Stone on the Hill. All morning long he'd tried to erase the vision of Abigale lifting her veil and revealing the deepest blue eyes he had ever seen. Why did she have to be the beautiful lass from the loch? Why did she have to be Abigale Bruce? It would be much easier to stay away from her if the lass had been an ugly hag, but she was far from a hag. Beauty like an angel, grace like a queen, and charm that could drive a man daft. How was he supposed to stay away when the lass tempted his willpower in such a way even he did not understand it?

I receive ye as mine. The words he'd uttered last eve haunted him.

"God's wounds."

He did not want to take a wife. Being a Guardian of Scotland, Dragonkine, there was only room for one woman in his life and it was Lady Scotland. Gut-wrenching reality hit… how was he going to tell Abigale about his other half? "Och lass, I forgot to tell ye, I'm a dragon and I spit fire." That should go over well. Nay, he would make sure Abigale never knew. Besides she wouldn't be staying long.

Agreeing to marry the king's daughter brought more bother to him than he bargained for, but then again the king of Scotland, Robert Bruce, had a sly way of sweetening the deal. Land. Even though James's home was in Angus, he did not own the land, so it was a perfect opportunity to set the stakes high. A bountiful dowry no man nor dragon could turn down.

After James was knighted a knight banneret on the battlefield; that was when the king had laid it on him.

"James, we have business to discuss." Robert Bruce slapped James on the shoulder and continued to walk. The king was one who waited for no one.

James peered up from the trencher piled high with vegetables and meats. No amount of hunger could stop his curiosity. Quickly he wiped his mouth, left the table and caught up with King Robert.

They made their way up to the king's solar. The king paced slowly, deep in thought in front of the hearth, with his hands behind his back. "Have ye gathered enough men in support of yer banner?" King Robert asked.

"Aye, yer Grace, enough to lead yer next quest."

"Verra good. Ye see, James, my next quest is verra special to me. I've gone to great lengths to ensure no one knows about it."

James stood tall, his stance confident. Intrigued by what King Robert was saying he listened intently.

"I am well prepared to pay ye generously for yer service, if ye shall agree to my terms."

"Service? Yer Grace, I already serve ye and ye have been more than generous to me."

"And ye have served me well." King Robert walked to his wooden desk, sat down and steepled his fingers. "I've always considered ye like a son. Yer father, God rest his soul, and me go way back. He would be proud of ye."

That couldn't be farther from the truth. How could a father approve of the vindictive ways his son conducted warfare or the way he dealt out brutality to those who stood in his way? Nay, far from proud his father would be, James thought.

"What of this quest ye seek?" James asked

Robert tapped his steepled fingers on his bearded chin. "I have someone verra precious to me, Abigale my daughter. I've arranged for her to be married."

James knew the king would only trust him and his men at arms to escort the princess of Scotland. This made perfectly good sense, but knowing the king as well as he did he still waited cautiously for his request.

"I've arranged for ye to make leave for Castle Douglas in the morn. There ye will marry my daughter."

The room started to spin and the air in his lungs seized. Sweat began to bead on his forehead and his palms went cold. Had the king gone daft? Robert Bruce knew what he was, yet he was willing to marry his daughter off to a dragon. "God's Teeth!" James wiped the sweat streaking down from his temple. He began to pace the small space in front of the king's desk.

Finally James gathered his thoughts before he did something daft himself like run down to the gallows and hang himself.

"Yer Grace, with all due respect, I can no marry yer daughter."

"'Tis a shame." Bruce paused and reached inside his desk drawer. He began to uncoil a scroll that appeared to have a map on it. "Angus is such a beautiful piece of land, tucked in between two huge lochs."

The king paused for a moment. "Tell me, James, how much coin do the oat fields bring in? Profitable, I assume?"

"Aye." James had been defeated. There was no way around it. The king always got what he wanted, one way or another. Also, there was that feeling of gratitude gnawing in his gut. He had to marry the king's daughter, for he owed a debt.

"So, prepare for travel?" Bruce asked.

"Aye."

"Good. This makes me a happy man." Then he began signing land documents over to James.

A generous and inviting dowry was too enticing to turn down. Marrying Abigale gained him not only Angus, but Bothwell Castle by the River Clyde in South Lanarkshire as well. But this newly owned land did not change the fact that James did not want a wife. But, with orders to take the princess to the safety of Angus and far away from the lowlands, James had to wonder if King Robert had other motives as well. *Why does he remove me from the battlefield? Send me to the Highlands to live the mundane life of a clan chief? God's Teeth! Am I more valuable behind a desk?*

Nay, he was one of the seven Guardians of Scotland, chosen to defend and protect Scotland like his fellow Dragonkine warriors. Plus his mind was sharp when it came to strategizing attacks, the best there was. The king could not afford to lose him on the battlefield.

Regardless of Robert's reasoning, he now had a wife. "A wife." He spat. A forceful hoof stomp and aggravated tail swish let James know he had tightened his saddle a little snug for his horse's liking. He rubbed his black mare on her chest. "Sorry, Lassie."

James patted the mare on her hindquarters as he walked behind her making his way toward the stable's entrance. He leaned his massive shoulder against the door frame of the stable and looked over at Castle Douglas. Rolling green hills now surrounded his land. He remembered a time when the castle was not so pleasant. It had been seized by English filth.

His family was outside the bailey's protective wooden staked wall, just far enough away from the brutal massacre of the Clan Douglas men. No familiar war cries were left. Only the blood-curdling sounds of the wounded being slain by the English army could be heard. Their clan had been on the verge of being defeated. Sir William, James's father and clan chief, had to make a decision and fast. The English army had fought hard and were closing in on them. An English victory for certain.

Sir William looked down, deeply, into his young son's eyes. A warrior-worn face bloodied and swollen, yet he was still a man in charge. "Son, do no fret or shed tears for me," Sir William demanded.

"Da, I bid ye, please let me stay and fight," wee James begged as he swiped at a fallen tear.

"Nay, Clan Douglas fought well, but the odds were against us. We have lost too many good men today. I must do what's right for our people."

James shook his head and tightened his fists. "Nay, we can still fight. This is our home."

Sir William bent down in front of his son and placed his hands on his shoulders. It was difficult for James to see his father this way; a broken man desperate to keep his family together. James raged inside just like the bloody war raging inside the walls of Castle Douglas.

"James, listen to me. Ye are the man of the family now." A sob from his wife caught his father's attention. William paused and looked up at her. His beautiful wife had fought so hard to hold back her tears but had failed. Her body trembled as she covered her mouth with her shaking hand to stifle another sob. She pulled their younger son of seven years close to her.

William turned his attention to his wee James. "Ye must take care of your mother and brother now."

Tears rushed down James's face as he shook his head in denial. His face reddened with anger. What a task to bear for a boy no more than ten winters old.

"Ye know the plan, get to Paris and there ye will be safe. Do ye understand me, lad?" Sir William commanded.

James's anger got the best of him. He was angry at his father for sending him away. He was angry at the English filth for ripping his family apart. He raged inside and began to erupt like a spewing volcano.

"*Ye are a coward!*" *James exploded and began to hit his father in the chest with tiny fists. "Coward!"*

William threw his arms around his raging son and hugged him tight as if he understood his son's outrage, for he seethed just the same inside.

The metal clang of knight mail and heavy marching feet grew near. There was no time to waste. If William wanted to keep his family safe he needed to say goodbye now. Their time together had come to an end.

Sir William let go of his son. James took a few steps back and stared at his father. No words were spoken between the two of them.

James watched his mother cry convulsively as she clung to the broken man. His little brother stood between his parents as if they were his shelter from this terrible nightmare. James's vision blurred and time slowed to a crawl. He looked around at the mayhem of bloodied warriors fighting and the destruction they left behind. Forever this day would be branded into his memories. He vowed he would come home and avenge his family's name.

William let go of his wife and walked over to a young Robert Bruce. He trusted only one man with his family and Robert, with his English connections, was the one who could get his family safely to Paris.

William clasped his hand on Robert's shoulder, "Bruce, ye make damn sure they're on that boat to Paris. Understood?"

"Aye."

James watched his father as he turned to face him. Standing tall, he took one last tender look at his family huddled together, tears streaking their faces. James knew this was his father's way of saying their final goodbye.

William nodded to Robert. "God speed, my friend."

With the last bit of pride William had he stood tall and smiled at his wife. Like a man on a mission he turned, unleashed his sword and ran back to the battle as he yelled one last war cry. "A Douglas! A Douglas!" As God was his witness he would take down a few more Sassenach filth before he surrendered his home.

James took a deep breath as he felt a tear threaten to fall. He would take his last breath slaying the English for taking everything from him. His father, his land, and his mother. His mother never got over losing his father. Some said she died of the plague, but he knew better; she died of a broken heart.

When James had returned to Scotland, several summers ago, he reclaimed his home from the English and avenged his family's name. As his eyes roamed to the west side of Castle Douglas, charred stone reminded him of that night. He and his force of three massive dragons beheaded the English garrison, torched them and decapitated their horses. It was the first time he had unleashed the wrath of his dragon, and he felt no remorse for the English scum. Even today, when the wind blew just right, the smell of burning flesh could still be detected.

He sent a message that day. From then on, he was known as the Black Douglas, the Bogeyman.

A soft female voice came from the rear of the stable and claimed his attention.

~~~~~

"Good Morn, Fergus." Abigale greeted her fine steed.

The brilliant white steed let out a welcoming nicker as Abigale approached.

"I've a surprise for ye," Abigale teased. Reaching into her pocket she pulled out a juicy red apple.

Ears pricked in her direction, he bobbed his head up and down as if he approved of her surprise.

Abigale offered the apple and held onto it as he took a bite. She found Fergus's favorite spot to be scratched, right between his ears, and gave him a good scratch.

"Ah, Fergus, what are we going to do?" Abigale sighed as if she carried the weight of the world on her shoulders.

After last eve's performance, Abigale had pondered most of the morning away as she ate stale oatcakes and picked at her black pudding. James had never returned, leaving her to a peaceful night's rest. Why had he showed her mercy? He was her husband now; certainly he had the right to bed his wife.

"That really is some kind of horse ye have."

Abigale jumped, surprised to find she wasn't alone. James was leaning his shoulder up against the stall with his arms crossed. "Ye frightened me." She held her hand over her chest to calm herself. "How long have ye been there… watching me?"

"Long enough." James pushed off the stall and grabbed a saddle nearby. "We leave for Angus soon. 'Tis best ye prepare for travel."

A crease appeared across her forehead. "I thought Castle Douglas was yer home?"

"Aye, it is. Archibald, my brother, will stay here to protect it. We head north." James tipped his chin toward the Highlands.

"The Highlands?"

James blew out a huff. "Aye."

Abigale followed closely behind as he sat the saddle down next to Fergus's stall. As he turned around she almost bumped into him. A cold stare sent chills over her skin causing her to take a step back. One look from those eyes made her feel so small, like a wee child.

"But it's dangerous to travel through the Highlands." She glanced down at her clasped hands nervously. "We would be much safer here."

"What's wrong lass, are ye afraid a rogue Highlander will jump out of the woods to attack ye?"

Abigale didn't take kindly to being teased. Being a woman and out on her own without the safety of the nunnery walls, she was apprehensive of traveling to the Highlands.

Abigale stood with her hands on her hips. "Ye see my Laird, I've only met one Highlander in my life and I'm no impressed." She looked him up and down.

Before she knew what was happening, James had closed the distance between them. Abigale felt giant hands grip her waist as she was pulled against a hard wall of muscle. Confused by his actions, she threw her hands to his chest in protest. She did not realize the repercussions of her actions.

As soon as their bodies connected, she felt his heat radiating off him. Amber eyes swirled leaving her breathless. She felt his cock harden against her stomach and instantly her body burned. He lowered his head. God help her, he was going to kiss her. She closed her eyes and waited for his kiss, but to her disappointment it never came.

Quickly she was hoisted up by her waist, only to open her eyes to find James setting her down off to the side and out of his way. He walked past her and lifted a bridle off of a hook as if she had no effect on him. "Ye best hold yer tongue, lass. I have no tolerance for it," he warned her.

Abigale stood dumbfounded. As sure as the sky was blue he was going to kiss her, she knew it. She felt it. Why did he stop? *Did I do something wrong?* She touched her lips and watched him walk over and grab the bridle like nothing had happened. This maddened her to no end. Threats and intimidation would not work on her; they only added fire to her fury. She had spent the last eight years surviving Abbess Margaret's mercilessness. Now that she was free from her ruthless behavior, Abigale wouldn't stand for the abuse.

"Is that the way ye Highlanders talk to yer wives?" Abigale bit back. "If so, my Laird, I'm still no impressed."

James strode in front of Abigale holding her blue stare of ire. "Lass, let's get one thing straight, I give the orders and ye are to obey."

Abigale felt her blood boil up to the tips of her ears as she grabbed her skirts to prevent herself from slapping him.

"I didnae want a wife. 'Tis best ye keep yer distance and do as yer told." James broke their stare and began to saddle up a mount.

Abigale didn't know where her courage came from, but this man was not going to get the best of her nor the satisfaction of knowing how furious he made her. Arrogant fool. "I see, my Laird 'tis best to be seen but not heard. Like a well-trained dog?"

James began to tighten the saddle. "See it as ye wish, just do as yer told." He brushed her off like an annoying fly buzzing around.

Before Abigale made her way back to Castle Douglas to pack for travel she sauntered next to James so he had to look at her."Yer an arse, James Douglas."

James smirked back and gave the saddle strap a good yank. "Now lass, is that any way to talk to yer husband?"

Abigale shot him a disgusted glare. She thought better than to exchange any more words so she turned on her heels and headed toward Castle Douglas to pack.

Chapter 5

A road less traveled...

The announcement that they were going to make camp for the night was music to Abigale's ears. Keeping up with five mountainous Highlanders as they rode their horses through the Highlands started to wear on her body. Breaks were few, short lived, and the rocky, rough terrain had wreaked havoc on her backside. James, determined to make it at least half way to Angus before nightfall, rode them hard. These men were accustomed to the land and their bodies were built to absorb the brutal beating the Highlands could bring upon a person, but she wasn't.

It was outlandish and well, plain rude to treat her like one of his men-at-arms. Though never once did she grumble about her discomfort. She rode with grace and kept to herself, but inside Abigale stewed.

I dinnae want a wife, James's voice rang through her thoughts. Abigale huffed and rolled her eyes. Did he really think she wanted to marry the Bogeyman? Nay, she was perfectly content back at the nunnery studying to become a surgeon and help heal the sick. Most nights she found herself nose deep in a book, reading up on herbs or looking over notes taken during an observed surgery. As long as she stayed clear of Abbess Margaret, life was, well... predictable, safe.

Who are you fooling, Abigale Bruce? She scolded herself. The nunnery was not the place she wanted to be. In fact as of late she had grown restless with images of wee bairns running amuck, calling her mother. A mother... just that thought warmed her inside. She wanted a husband to call a friend, a lover who could make her toes curl with one kiss. Aye, she sighed, a family. A family like she had never known. Now that desire seemed to crumble away to nothing more than a wishful dream. *I dinnae want a wife.*

The more she pondered the more blame she placed on James. He'd made it perfectly clear she was nothing more than a nuisance… a bump in the road… a thorn in his backside. Well, she would show him who the thorn was, she thought. At this point, she could not decide what burned her arse more, James or the bloody saddle.

"We'll camp here for the night," James announced.

Abigale winced when they came to a halt. Dismounting was going to be a challenge; she had no feeling left in her legs.

James hopped down off of his black mare and looked for a place to set up camp while two of his men went to search for wood to build a fire. Abigale noticed how he commanded his men and the way they respected him. A true natural born leader indeed. She respected him for that, but his manners on the other hand, well, not so much.

After she realized she was on her own, Abigale slowly slid off from the saddle onto numb, stinging legs. Pain crept across her face as she steadied herself against Fergus. The white steed turned his head and nudged her with his wet nose as if he asked how she fared. Patting him on his head, she smiled and reassured him that she was fine.

Desperately needing to set up a spot so she could get some rest, she began to untie a rolled up blanket and fur. As she took her first step, her legs buckled. Strong arms caught her from behind before she hit the hard ground.

"Ye alright, lass?" James asked.

"*Are ye alright?*" What kind of question was that? Of course she was not alright; her backside throbbed and her legs stung. She was exhausted, famished, and in desperate need of a bath. Besides she really did not want his help. She would be fine on her own, just like she had been her whole life. Alone.

"I'm fine." Abigale brushed him off and tried to walk away only to stumble back into his arms.

"Here, let me help. Ye can take my pallet." Before Abigale could protest, James scooped her up in his strong arms and walked her over to his pallet.

He sat her gently down on soft fur then reached into a satchel and handed her an oatcake. "Here, eat this."

Taking the oatcake, Abigale eyed him curiously. "Thank ye."

Abigale ate in silence. Wondering why he was treating her with kindness, she watched him keenly. Walking back to the black mare, he retrieved a waterskin. Oh thank Heavens… water. She was parched.

"Drink this," James demanded.

Abigale gladly took the skin and drank vigorously. A strong overbearing taste burned her throat and her stomach threatened to lurch. She spat out the amber liquid and coughed.

James smirked. "What's wrong? Have ye no had whiskey before?"

Abigale shot him a cross glance as she wiped her mouth off on her sleeve. "Nay. 'Tis awful."

"'Tis an acquired taste, but trust me it will help."

After the wretched liquid settled in her stomach, Abigale watched James tend to the fire. Why was he being nice to her? It remained apparent that he had thought nothing of her wellbeing throughout the day and showed no mercy.

She was growing quite fond of this side of James; the caring, gentle side. It made her wonder why he didn't want a wife. From what she'd viewed, he'd showed kindness, in his own way, she supposed. He was honorable, which she knew, because of his loyalty to her father. However, what could have happened to make this Highland warrior not want to take a wife?

At times he seemed to be far away, deep in thought. Perhaps a love gone bad or had he lost a love? If unlucky in love, she could understand wanting to protect your heart from the pain. Then again, what did she know? She had never been in love. What a mystery this man was to her.

She felt her skin prick and her body warmed. Looking up, her eyes met an amber glare. She swallowed hard past the lump in her throat. She'd been found out, for James now stood over her with his arms crossed over his chest.

"What?" James stood firm.

Quickly, she looked down into her lap, not wanting to make eye contact. "'Tis nothing."

"Lass, say what's on yer mind before ye worry yer bottom lip off."

Abigale sighed in defeat. She had been told before that she was easy to read. Sister Kate had voiced that many times. *Abigale Bruce, ye wear yer heart on yer sleeve.* Surprisingly, Abigale wished Sister Kate was here now. She needed her words of wisdom, now more than ever.

She looked up at the towering warrior. "Why do ye no want a wife?"

James clenched his jaw as if this question irritated him. "Abigale, get some rest." He began to walk off toward his horse.

"My Laird, if I may—"

James stopped abruptly and turned to face her. "Nay, ye may not."

"It's just... ye've been kind and —"

49

"Lass, dinnae mistake my concern for yer wellbeing as an act of kindness." Sternness swept across his face. "I'm no the monster everyone makes me oot to be."

Abigale knew better than to push the issue, so she let him walk away. She took the skin and sipped; this time the whiskey didn't taste as bad. Welcoming the warmth of the liquid, she snuggled deep into the furs and lost herself in her thoughts. Sooner or later she would crack open the mystery.

~~~~~

The last purple hue in the sky disappeared beyond the horizon as dusk quickly turned into night. The chattering of night creatures filled the air, a raging fire flickered and crackled in the center of camp. James sat propped up against a weeping willow tree where he'd spent most of the night watching Abigale. It wasn't long after the second sip of whiskey that her eyelids grew heavy with sleep. Deeply nestled inside the furs, she looked like an angel. Long dark eye lashes rested on her flawless cheeks, her mouth was slightly open, and James could hear her soft breaths. She mesmerized him, enticed him.

Furthermore, he found it quite enjoyable to sit and watch. The vision of Abigale talking to Fergus back at the stables brought a smile to his face. The way her face lit up, the soft touches she gave Fergus, even the way she bit her bottom lip when she was deep in thought captivated him. He cursed silently. *Was he really becoming jealous of a horse?*

Abigale sighed, bringing James's attention back to the beauty sleeping right before him. Soft curves called to him as she nuzzled deeper into the furs. His body ached as he fought the urge to slide under the covers and press his body against hers. His hands twitched with the thought of running them over her breasts, down her stomach and… Before he knew it, he licked his lips. *How sweet she would taste.*

He scrubbed his hands down his face like he was trying to erase her from his thoughts. No such luck. With his bastard of a dragon stirring inside, the beast purred in agreement. God's teeth, he should have claimed her when he had the chance to. Surely it would make his decision to send her away a lot easier.

A rant from Rory grabbed his attention. One last look at Abigale and James made his way to where his men were sitting around the fire. He hadn't joined his fellow Dragonkine yet. To be honest he didn't want to hear about the short-heeled wenches they had been with or their recent tavern brawls. Nay, James had other things on his mind.

"I dinnae understand –"

"Understand what?" James interrupted Rory as he approached the site.

"My Laird, I'm afraid Rory has had a wee drop too much mead and is loose with his tongue." Conall eyed Rory as if telling him to shut it.

"I have nay." Rory became defensive. "Ye know 'tis true, humans have their rightful king. Why can't we have our king?" Rory drained the last of his mead.

Magnus, an elder Dragonkine, spoke up, answering Rory's question. "Aye lad, at one time we did have our own king who ruled along with King MacAlpin. Dragonkine flourished in our own kingdom." Magnus had a faraway look on his face, as if he remembered that time very well. "Aye, many glorious years of peace."

Rory gazed at Magnus. "Until we became a threat."

"'Tis true, King MacAlpin slaughtered our people along with our king, King Drest," Conall stated.

"Aye, it was supposed to be a peaceful meeting between kings and our royal seven. Ale, food, and women aplenty were offered as the kings made peace. So we thought. Before King Drest and our royals knew what was happening, the floors to the great hall had opened up sending our people deep underground. Bodies impaled upon sharp spikes, they couldn't move, and the trap doors on the floor were sealed shut. Covered with earth, our king and royals were buried alive." Magnus paused, clearing his throat. "Only a few Dragonkine survived that day." Magnus stared into the flickering flames as if he saw the past recurring.

"I dinnae call surrendering surviving," Rory bit back.

After the dreadful massacre King MacAlpin had showed no mercy to the Kine. The king's orders were to slay every Dragonkine in the realm, man, woman, or child, it did not matter. As the last remaining seven Kine warriors stood with cold steel pressed against their necks and arms and legs bound with chains, King MacAlpin changed his mind. Mayhap the last seven remaining would come in handy as he looked onward to battling future enemies. A massive, powerful dragon on his or any future human king's side would be of great value.

So, an agreement had been made. There would only be seven Dragonkine warriors left to roam the Earth, all warriors would be ruled by Scottish kings and become Guardians of Scotland. When called upon, they were to fight for the greater good. When one Kine died another would take its place, chosen by the dragon elders. Rory had a point; surrendering was not surviving.

With no more freedom to sustain, a species will either die or become accustomed to their new surroundings. Well, being immortal left you with only one option, adapt. As time would tell, some Dragonkine had a hard time with this. Most warriors' dragons were bloodthirsty with revenge, so being on the battlefield killing humans sufficed their carnal need, good or bad. Morals didn't count as long as there was blood shed. Being endless came with another burden for some; falling in love with a human woman. If a woman could overcome the idea that she loved a dragon, she would become immortal as long as her mate was alive. Because most women rejected a Kine's dragon side, most warriors protected their hearts and vowed to never fall in love.

As James thought further about the history of the ancients, the downfall of their kingdom, he knew what the feud between the kings was about; a woman. "King MacAlpin's son fell in love with King Drest's daughter. If they were to have married the next male heir would have become the Dragonkine king and king of Scotland. One king to rule both realms."

"Nay my friend, ye have it all wrong." Rory stalked over to James to make his point clear. "It was about King MacAlpin's greed. He wanted to rule Dragonkine and humans. We became a threat. MacAlpin killed our people in order to be king of both realms." Rory seethed with hatred.

"'Tis enough, Rory," James warned. He could feel the tension rising and nothing good ever came from sparring dragons.

"Nay, think about it. There are seven of our Kine left, for three of the seven we have no clue where they are. James, 'tis not natural for Dragonkine to live in a human world. We need our women to calm our dragons. If we had our own king ye would no have had to marry her." Rory pointed in Abigale's direction.

James could feel his anger as it started to rage inside, for he knew Rory had a point. But the past was the past. The king of Scotland held his loyalty. "Abigale is of no concern to ye," James bit back.

Conall stood, prepared to break up a nasty fight. "Indeed it is the past." He peered sternly at Rory.

Both James and Rory stood eye to eye, nostrils flared as they waited for someone to make a move.

"Enough." Magnus's deep demanding voice rang out. "'Twas long ago. We have mended those old wounds and our king is the king of Scotland."

"But old wounds have left deep scars, Magnus, ye cannae deny it," Rory stated as he held James's stare.

Magnus stretched as he stood, breaking up the standoff between the warriors. "Lads I'll take first watch." He walked toward his pallet; indeed old wounds left deep scars.

~~~~~

Abigale tossed and turned, eventually awaking to a throbbing pain throughout her backside; her skin burned and muscles ached. The few sips of whiskey had helped some, but no matter which way she turned, she could not ease the pain. As she lay on her side she remembered seeing a clump of low-growing purple flowers, self-heal. She had just read about its ability to help heal wounds and soothe bruises. She needed to find that plant.

Rhythmic, thunderous snoring belted through the night, as four massive Highlanders with their mouths open and bodies limp surrounded the campsite. Their boisterous snores could have wakened the dead. Perfect timing to search for that plant, she thought. No one would know she was gone. Abigale sat up and stretched her stiff legs before she made an effort to stand.

Thankful she had feeling back in her legs, she walked gingerly toward the woodland's edge away from camp. Not remembering exactly where she had seen the plant last, she went deeper. The forest came alive as the fullness of the moon shined down over the trees, casting eerie shadows throughout the glen; frogs croaked and small nocturnal animals rustled in the undergrowth. As she passed an old tree, an owl hooted, causing her to jump. She shook her head at herself and laughed. *Abigale, ye big chicken, 'tis only an owl, for heaven's sake.* But still the darkness gave her the creeps.

She continued her search through every blade of grass, every clump of flowers, but came up empty handed. If it wasn't for the constant throbbing, she would have given up. It had to be around here somewhere; she had seen it. Hope of finding her precious flower started to fade and so did her energy.

Walking over towards the loch she noticed, from the corner of her eye, a purple flower. The moon lit the flower as if it was glowing. A smile crossed her lips as she stopped and picked a few petals from the plant.

~~~~~

Sleep always avoided James. Plagued with recurring nightmares, he preferred not to sleep. As of late the dreams had become all too real. Death was coming for him, he felt it deep in his bones. Rolling over on his back, frustrated, he cursed. Even the Bogeyman had demons nipping at his heels.

James pushed aside his thoughts and decided a dip in the nearby loch would calm his nerves. He looked over at the clump of furs where Abigale slept. She looked to be deeply snuggled and resting comfortably. He couldn't see her beautiful auburn head, for she must have hidden in the furs to drown out the snores. Aye, a quick dip in the cold loch would clear his head.

As James approached the loch, he came across a small figure leaning against a boulder. Not being able to make out the image, he pulled out his dirk and crouched down. As he drew closer, the clouds in the dark sky shifted just enough to shed light upon the object.

"Abigale?" His forehead creased in confusion. "What are ye doing out here, lass?"

"James? I thought ye were sleeping." She stood, trying not to show how much pain she was in.

"Answer my question." He crossed his massive arms in front of his chest. "What are ye doing out here?"

"I couldn't sleep, so I decided to take a walk."

He didn't believe her. No way would a lass be out here in the dark just to take a stroll. It was too dangerous. The glen was known for its abundance of wild boar, and when approached, the beasts could be quite nasty. Aye, she was hiding something from him; she was a horrible liar. "What's that in yer hand?" He reached for the purple petals, but quickly she hid them behind her back.

"Nothing. 'Tis my business."

"Abigale, I'm in no mood for games." James stepped forward then grabbed the flower from behind her.

"Give it back!" She yanked the flower from his hands. "Ye have no right coming out here telling me what to do. Ye told me to keep my distance, now ye keep yers," she demanded.

He noticed Abigale was uneasy on her feet when she tried to take a step away from him. She had swayed, lost her balance, and grabbed ahold of the boulder to steady herself.

Went for a walk my arse, James thought. The lass was in too much pain.

Hunched over, Abigale supported her weight with both hands on the boulder. Long auburn hair hung loosely over the sides of her face. Indeed she was in a great deal of pain. "What ails ye?" He brushed her hair away from her face so he could see her.

She looked up at him and her blue eyes stole his breath away. "Nothing. I'll be fine."

Even in pain the lass couldn't be more beautiful, yet he was beginning to find out that she was as stubborn as he was. "Lass, ye dinnae look fine. Now, let me help." Looking down he noticed a trail of blood running down her leg. "Yer bleeding." Concerned, James grabbed her skirts and frantically started to push them up her thigh. He needed to know where the blood was coming from.

"Enough... enough." She swatted at his hands. "I'll let ye help if ye let go of my skirt." Abigale surrendered.

"Fine." In one fast motion James grabbed her under dress and ripped a strip off. "I'll be right back. Dinnae move. I'm going to the loch for some water."

~~~~~

"Dinnae move." Abigale repeated his words silently. Where did he think she was going to go? If she could she would run away and hide, for this was going to be the most humiliating night of her life. There was no way she was going to accept his help. First of all she was madder than a wet hen at him and secondly she was not going to let him rub self-heal on her buttocks. She would make do somehow, as soon as she got rid of him.

Clearing moss from a spot on the boulder, Abigale began to crush the petals into a paste. It was not ideal, but at this point she could care less. She needed relief.

James quickly returned from the loch and began to lift Abigale's skirts.

"Wait I —"

"Lass, I'm just going to wipe the blood off and see where it's coming from."

Clearly he wasn't going to take no for an answer, so there was no need to hold on to the last bit of dignity she had left. They locked eyes and she could see his true concern for her. Slowly she gathered her skirts and turned around until her bare, ruby red bottom was exposed.

James grabbed her hips, moved her toward the moonlight, and bent down behind her. She heard a sigh, but James did not say a word.

Finally Abigale looked over her shoulder. "How bad is it?"

"Well lass, ye have a bad case of saddle sores. One of the blisters has opened and that's where the blood is coming from."

Ever so gently, James began to dab away at the blood. Abigale hissed when he swiped the wet fabric over the injured skin. She felt a cool breeze against her skin and it wasn't from the night air. *Did he just blow on my bottom?*

It wasn't long before the pain started to dull. Abigale leaned her head back and stared into the starry night sky. Could this night get any worse? She was mortified standing here naked from the waist down. It seemed as of late, every time James was around, a part of her body was naked. Surely, he must be repulsed by the look of her bottom. She wished she could pray this night away.

James stood and helped straighten Abigale's skirts. Humiliated, Abigale hid her face in her hands. She didn't want to look at him; how could she? Little by little James had seen her naked. Not only was she physically exposed, but she felt just as naked emotionally. She was slowly being stripped away from everything she had ever known. No longer was her life predictable like back at the nunnery. Her whole world had been turned upside down and now her future lay in the hands of a man who did not want her. Maybe it was exhaustion taking over or perhaps emotions were getting the best of her; whatever it might be, tears started to streak her beautiful face.

Strong hands pried her hands away from her face. James placed a finger under her chin lifting her head back until their eyes met.

"Och lass, don't cry." James wiped a tear from her cheek. "Ye have the finest arse I've ever seen." He smirked.

Abigale laughed through her tears and swatted at his chest playfully. "Dinnae make me laugh. I'm mad at ye."

Gently James picked her up and cradled her in his arms. "I guess I deserve that much."

As they made their way back to the campsite, Abigale laid her head on his shoulder and lost herself in sleep.

Chapter 6

Only the very brave and the very foolish enter the dragon's lair.

"My lady, ye best be gettin' up."

Abigale awoke to a plump older woman with light brown hair streaked with gray, creating a commotion. Forcefully, the woman removed the furs from the small window letting in a ray of sunlight. With much irritation, Abigale quickly threw the covers over her head and turned her body to block the cursed light.

The overbearing woman grabbed the sheets from the bottom of Abigale's bed and ripped them off her body. "Ye cannae stay in bed all day. Now, up with ye before I get the bucket of cold water."

Abigale struggled to open her eyes as she stretched her stiff, sleep stricken body. Slowly a bedchamber she didn't recognize came into view. In a frenzy, she straightened herself in to a sitting position as she looked around the room for some clue to where she was. Unfamiliar tapestries hung from the gray stone walls. One of the tapestries showed a gruesome battle scene. *Wait...* Abigale rubbed the sleep from her eyes. *Is that a dragon fighting in the tapestry?* Shaking that thought she noticed a huge fire burning in the hearth that filled one side of the room and the smell of lavender lingered in the air. *A bath,* she sighed.

As Abigale scooted to the edge of the bed, visions of days past clouded her memory. Looking down at her hand, she caressed her thumb across the golden band. The wedding was not a dream, but a reality. A dull tingle on her backside reminded her of the long travel and... oh no. Humiliation washed over her. James had tended to her wounds.

Abigale shot out of bed and ran over to the mirror that stood in the corner of the room. Quickly she lifted her night-gown, turned around, and looked over her shoulder at her buttocks. Amazed at what she saw, she rubbed her hand across one butt cheek; soft, pink healing skin covered the blisters and she felt no pain just a dull ache. *How could she have healed so fast? How long had she been asleep?*

"Oh my lady, forgive me. Ye're in pain from yer travels, aye?" Quickly Abigale dropped her gown and turned to face the woman.

"Come lass, I have a bath waiting for ye." The woman gently led Abigale toward the bath and patted her arm, reassuring her. "The warmth will help ease the pain."

Without a doubt this woman was in charge of the castle and took her job quite seriously, for she had a firm but caring way about her. Thank God because if she had to deal with another Griselda she would go daft. "Where am I?"

"Black Stone on the Hill, my lady."

Black Stone? Aye, she was traveling to Black Stone, but why could she not remember how she got here? She remembered everything up until James picked her up and carried her back to the campsite. Ironically she'd forgotten the whole trip to Black Stone. *Strange, I must have blacked out from exhaustion,* she mused.

Abigale walked with the kind woman over to the tub. Steam rose along with the scent of lavender from the inviting water. *Heaven awaits.*

"And how long have I been asleep?"

"Two days, lass."

"Two days?" She'd been asleep for two days? How could this be?

The woman began to pull off Abigale's night-gown. Abigale stepped back and pushed the woman's hands away.

"A wee bit shy are we?" The woman turned her back to give Abigale some privacy.

Abigale gathered up her night-gown and pulled it off over her head. Dipping a toe into the water, she tested its warmth. The water felt heavenly as she lowered herself into the tub. After a few seconds she relaxed and allowed her body to absorb the heat.

The woman held out a bar of soap and pointed at Abigale's hair. "May I?"

Abigale wasn't fond of this type of treatment; she had to make do on her own back at the abbey. Abbess Margaret had made sure of that. The last punishment Abigale received was one of the cruelest and most painful. Indeed it had to be that Abbess Margaret knew Abigale was going to be leaving the nunnery soon, so she had one last punishment to give. The Abbess couldn't use tether on her flesh, nor leave bruises, it would leave a mark and everyone would know of her mistreating Abigale. This left her long auburn hair as the weapon of choice.

Late one night, she had awoken to the dreadful woman coiling Abigale's hair around her hand as if she was in a daze. "Ye think yer pretty don't ye, bastart?" Abigale kept silent until she was yanked out of bed by her hair, dragged down to the church, and forced to pray to be forgiven for all the sins she had been accused of committing.

Honestly Abigale didn't want to be touched by anyone, but she felt like she could trust this woman. "Aye," she smiled meekly.

Working the soap into a lather, the woman let out a soft chuckle. "Dinnae worry, it will be over before ye know it."

"What will be over?" Abigale was confused.

"Aye, ye are a married woman now. Yer husband will want to bed his wife."

Abigale laughed silently to herself. Apparently this woman didn't know how James felt about her and the whole marriage arrangement. He'd made that perfectly clear. *I dinnae want a wife*, she mocked to herself. Then just like a change in the wind Abigale's thoughts turned on her. Back at Castle Douglas they had made everyone believe that they had consummated their marriage. Obviously, this woman knew differently.

"How do ye know we haven't… ye know… already?"

The woman got up and retrieved a pitcher. "Lass, yer secret is safe with me."

And she did believe her secret was safe, for the gray-haired woman had showed her more kindness than anyone had recently. She had a kind approachable way about her and Abigale felt as if she could trust her.

Abigale bit her bottom lip with worry and let out a shaky breath. "I've nae been with a man." Looking down at her hands she nervously picked at her nails. "I've heard it hurts."

"Aye lass, but only for a wee bit. Dinnae worry yer pretty head aboot it." Reaching over, the woman grabbed a pitcher full of fresh water. "Now, lean back so I can rinse the soap out yer hair."

Abigale leaned her head back and looked up at the woman. "I'm no used to all this fuss."

"Yer the lady of the hoose… of course we will fuss over ye. Besides I like ye." The woman winked at her and gave her a warm smile like a mother would give a child.

Recalling the last eight years, she'd benefitted from being the king's daughter and look where that had gotten her. Multiple tongue lashings and extra duties. There was no royal treatment for her; princess was just a given title. Abigale guessed she should be thankful. Even though she was a bastard, her father had recognized her as his own and that was a blessing in its own right. Nay, she would be treated like everyone else.

"I dinnae expect any special treatment. I'm no much of a cook, but I can help."

The woman clucked her tongue. "There's no need to help—"

"I insist," Abigale said firmly.

"Well then, ye are the lady, so if that's yer wish then—"

"It is."

After a few moments of silence the woman stood. "I'll leave a fresh gown out for ye and I'll be back with some food." She started to leave the wash area when Abigale called out, "Wait, yer name!"

The woman turned around and faced Abigale. "Me name is Alice."

Tears started to fill Abigale's eyes. "Thank ye Alice for being so kind to me."

Alice gave her the warmest smile, giving Abigale hope. Hope that mayhap she would find happiness here at Black Stone on the Hill.

~~~~~

"I've no met a princess before," Effie confessed as she blew a ringlet of bright red hair from her eye.

"Effie, I think ye have washed that plate clean." Alice was quite aware how nervous Effie was of meeting Abigale. Word had spread fast that the princess of Scotland was here and now wed to their clan's chief.

Drying off the spotless plate Effie turned to Alice who was preparing the nightly feast. The whole clan was coming together tonight in celebration of the return of their chief and his new bride.

"Alice, is she pretty? I wonder how many wonderful fairytale stories she has about growing up in royalty." Indeed, Effie was day dreaming herself about a prince charming and a happily ever after.

"Effie!" Alice scolded, "Keep yer head out of the clouds, lass. There is much work to be done. Grab that basket of carrots and start choppin'." Effie sauntered over to the basket and began her kitchen duty.

Abigale followed the chatter she heard coming from the kitchen, but paused and took a deep breath before she entered. She was not keen on kitchen duties, in fact she hated to cook. It never failed that she burned everything she tried to make. Not wanting to set a bad first impression with her cooking skills, Abigale hoped that Alice wouldn't ask her to cook.

"Awe lass, come in… come in." Alice welcomed her with open arms.

A luscious redhead dropped a knife and dashed over to Abigale, swiftly wiping her hands on her tattered apron. "My lady." She did her best curtsy trying to impress the princess.

"Please, no need to be formal with me." Abigale brushed off the formality. However, Abigale was surprised that she knew her true identity. Indeed she knew she was safe here, besides this was why her father had arranged this union between her and the Black Douglas, to keep her safe. A savage reputation like his, no one would dare try to harm her.

Abigale wondered where James was. Alas it had been two days since the last she saw him. She couldn't shake this feeling like something was missing, as if she wasn't whole. Well, she did know darn well who was missing and she longed to see him. "Alice? Where is Laird Douglas?"

"He's out in the bailey somewhere sparring with his men. They should be back midday," Alice confirmed.

"Oh." Abigale, a little disappointed, was hoping to see James sooner.

Most of the morning passed by quickly, as Alice attempted to teach Abigale how to make bread and prepare the night's feast. Nonetheless, it wasn't an easy task. Abigale just wasn't a good cook. Not for the lack of trying; she kneaded the dough just like Alice instructed, but the blasted sticky paste stuck to the table and all over her hands. To top it off the bread turned out hard as a rock, completely inedible.

"Dinnae fash lass, 'tis only yer first try. We can cut up the bread and use it for trenchers," Alice said.

A blast of laughter exploded between the women. God bless Alice for having the patience of a saint. Both women had made her feel right at home and she truly enjoyed their company. As they worked washing vegetables and chopping herbs, Alice and Effie had enlightened her about castle Black Stone and its clan members. For instance, there was a chapel near the castle where services were held regularly. The smith not only was a master behind his anvil, he also had a way with the lasses. There was a healer, with an exceptional gift, always on call. Then there were the men… Highlanders. Rogues, rascals up to no good, but without a doubt, they defended their clan with honor and with their lives. Though as Alice explained more about them, Abigale had a feeling Alice was highly respected by them and that they gave her no troubles.

After the kitchen disaster and almost setting her second loaf of bread to flames, Abigale, Effie, and Alice retired to the great hall. A savory aroma filled the air indicating that a variety of wild game was cooking in the kitchen. Servants scurried about arranging the great hall for tonight's feast as Clan Douglas welcomed home their chief and his new bride. Assorted wild flowers littered the tops of wooden tables, cobwebs had been dusted off the chandelier, and rugs of bright colors covered the stone floor. Tapestries hung high and draped the walls, and candlelight shining from the sconces illuminated the room giving it a golden glow. The great hall looked fit for a king.

The women took their seats next to the hearth where baskets full of clothes sat and waited to be mended. Soft leather boots needed new laces, tunics needed patching and trews needed stitching. "Alice, do all of these items belong to James?" Abigale couldn't imagine that a man like James would possess such a large amount of clothing.

"Nay, as a clan we take care of our people. So, when our men come home from battle, we mend what needs to be mended." Alice handed her a bloodstained tunic.

Abigale studied the stain for a while, her brows creased as she wondered who had worn this tunic and if they had lived to see another day. That stain represented so much more than just a stain. It was a reminder of just how unstable Scotland was. Brave men and women had lost their lives fighting for their freedom from the English. As if that wasn't enough, clan fought against clan, brother against brother, blood against blood. *When would the fighting stop?* she thought. She had seen and healed so many wounded men and saw too many of them die. Life was valuable to her and needed to be cherished, not destroyed.

The sound of heavy paws trampling through the great hall broke Abigale from her thoughts. Through the doorway bounded two huge, gray Scottish deerhounds. The beasts ran past her with their tongues hanging from the sides of their mouths in exhaustion. As if it were routine, they plopped down next to the hearth panting. Men jesting and laughing boisterously followed.

"Magnus old man, I think ye have lost yer touch," a blond-haired man boasted and shoved Magnus with his shoulder.

"Or he's still drunk with mead," Another man blurted out.

"Ye may outwit me with yer fancy blades, but I'd behead ye with one swing of my axe." Magnus's rough voice boomed over their laughter.

Abigale's heart stopped as James approached them. His long black hair stuck to his neck and bare chest with sweat, his kilt hung low on his hips, and his pectorals twitched slightly as if he was relieving sore muscles. God help her, this man was truly beautiful.

Smiling from ear to ear James strode over to Alice. "My dear Alice." He leaned down and placed a soft kiss on her cheek. "Och, how I've missed ye, bonny lass."

Alice dismissed his greeting with a swish of her hand. "My Laird, ye know how to make a lady blush."

For a moment Abigail envied Alice, for she wished James would look at her the way he looked at the older woman.

James glanced at Abigail and greeted Effie with a nod.

"I'll be in my bedchamber." James headed for the stone and iron staircase.

Alice scolded James like a child, "Nay so fast… aren't ye going to introduce yer men to yer lady?"

James rubbed the back of his neck and turned back to his men, who now stood in perfect line formation in front of Abigale like proper Highland soldiers. James shook his head.

"My apologies. This is Rory Cameron, my cousin Marcus Stewart, Conall Hamilton, and the handsome man in red is Magnus."

Magnus grunted and rolled his eyes in response to James's jest. "It be me pleasure to meet ye, my lady."

Abigale remembered Magnus from the campsite, but was never introduced properly. Magnus had long, unruly red hair, which was a shade lighter than his full beard that hung past his chin. Though they all seemed to look about the same age, Magnus seemed to have an authoritative demeanor.

Rory smoothed his hand through his shoulder-length blonde hair trying to tame the waves. As he approached Abigale, his eyes shimmered a bright blue when he smiled at her. "My lady." He knelt down without losing eye contact with her. *What a charmer, with a gaze like Rory's the lasses must swoon over him,* Abigale thought.

A deep rich voice broke her trance as Conall approached her. "Lady Abigale. 'Tis nice to be formally introduced." A scattered mess of chocolate curls, wet with sweat, hung just below his ears. He bent down and reached for her hand and kissed it. He was pure dominance in the same way James was, but seemed approachable.

"Aye, I do remember ye. Ye were my escort to the kirk?"

"Aye." He winked.

The noises in the hall must have obscured her hearing because she could have sworn she heard a growl coming from James.

After Conall finished his greeting with Abigale he set his blue-gray stare on Effie, and with a sly, sexy smile he turned Effie's freckled cheeks three shades of red. The lass quickly looked down at the leather boot she was re-lacing.

Marcus stood where he was and gave a nod.

A chill raced down Abigale's spine as Marcus glared skeptically at her. She hadn't noticed him on her travels to Black Stone, but the others she remembered. Abigale turned her attention back to James who was watching her intently with that piercingly protective stare.

"I'll be in my bedchamber." And with no other words James turned on his heels and ascended the stairs two at a time until he reached the loft that circled the great hall. Abigale watched him until he disappeared down a long corridor leading to their… his bedchamber.

Chapter 7

There is no room for two dragons in one pond. ~ Chinese Proverb

Softly stroked notes from a golden harp gracefully filled the great hall. A few hundred members of Clan Douglas were scattered around long wooden tables as they ate the night's feast. Chatter amongst them started up again as they finished the last of the wide variety of roasted game and vegetables.

James sat with his men and pondered how much his life was going to change now that he was home and had a wife. After an impressive victory at Bannockburn, James and his soldiers had sent King Edward the Second fleeing back to England, leaving behind a routed English army, and now he was home. It had been a while since James and his Dragonkine warriors had been back to Black Stone on the Hill. The battlefield had been the bane of their existence for God knew how long. Accepting his immortality was going to be a challenge; knowing that time was nonexistent in his world he was going to have a hard time adjusting to the solitude of a mundane life. At least if he was on the field time didn't seem to matter and his dragon's bloodlust was appeased. Furthermore, clan life was uninteresting to him. Surely, he should be securing the borders south of Stirling, but instead he was home and having a hard time adapting to the idea of solitude and a wife.

There was no more fighting for him, at least not on the battlefield. The king had made it clear that he was to protect his daughter and if that meant accepting clan life, James would do it.

James sat across from Conall and Magnus at the tables. Rory sat next to him working on his third trencher of food. Rory's body leaned forward over his treasure, his strong arms caging the dish like a dog guarding a bone.

Magnus and Conall sat with creased brows as they witnessed Rory's attack on a leg of mangled meat.

Magnus shook his red head in wonderment. "That laddie has one hell of a long stomach."

Conall took a long vigorous chug of mead then set the empty tankard on the table. "Aye, 'tis like watching a wild beast devour its prey. Repulsive."

Juices from the mangled leg dripped from the corners of Rory's mouth as he looked up from his trencher. His mouth full of food, he mumbled, "Ye can talk rubbish all ye want but I need my strength if I intend to be betwixt a lass's legs all night." He winked.

"Poor lass," Conall snickered.

James was oblivious to the nonsense chatter. A stunning woman in a royal blue dress had caught his attention the moment she came into view. As soon as he spotted Abigale he couldn't tear his eyes away from her. A tight bodice enhanced her breasts just enough to tease his eyes. Long waves of auburn hair danced across her shoulders as she sat and told a story to a group of twelve children. Like a warm ray of sunshine, her face lit up with a smile as she engaged the group of wee bairns. She was born to be a mother, he thought.

It had been too long since the last time he'd seen Abigale. On their way back to the campsite, James had used his magic to put her under a healing sleep that lasted for two days. It was the least he could do, for he was the cause of her discomfort. While on horseback, Abigale had rode draped across his lap as he held her tightly. Tiny as she was, she had fit perfectly tucked up next to him, soft curves snuggled against vigorous strength. For a moment he had wished he could hold her like that forever, but reality was bloody cruel.

"Ye have yerself one bonny wife." Conall nodded his head toward Abigale and brought James's attention to him.

James cleared his throat. "Aye." He picked up his tankard and drank heavily.

"So, when are ye going to have wee bairns of yer own running round the castle?" Conall jested.

Amber liquid shot from James's mouth and splattered all over Conall. "Bloody hell, Conall!"

"What?" Conall wiped the mead from his face and tunic, "Lady Abigale is a beauty, why no?"

"Look at her one more time and I'll rip yer eyes right out of their sockets." James didn't know why he threatened his brother at arms like that. The more he thought about Abigale, the more his world spun out of control.

"Nay, don't fash yerself, my friend." A luscious redhead playing the harp came into Conall's view.

~~~~~

Twelve children, between three and twelve years of age, bright-eyed, and curiously enthralled listened closely to Abigale as she told a tale about a brave knight who fought for Scotland's freedom. Leaning forward toward the children, she made sure the cherub-faced bairns paid close attention.

"And as the brave knight returned home from battle, he crept up the stairs to his daughter's bedchamber to bid her a good night. When he entered the room his daughter jumped out of bed and ran to her da. He pulled his little princess close and hugged her firmly. He made a vow that night as he said, 'do no fret my pet for ye shall be free. No longer shall ye be caged like a bird. Be free and fly, songbird.'"

Abigale paused for a moment. Remembering this story brought up the past. It was the same tale she told herself every night while living at Dunfermline Abbey.

Wee children rushed her as their lean arms hugged her neck. Wet kisses pecked her face, and Abigale returned their love with hugs of her own. "Now go play, and Niven, stay oot of Alice's special oatcakes." She waved an authoritative finger at him. "She'll have yer backside."

"Aye, my lady." Niven bowed.

Abigale sat there for a while as she watched the children scamper off. Niven was always getting into some kind of mischief. At least two times this morn he had snuck two oatcakes, and had been chased out of the kitchen by Alice several times by midday. That one there was a handful, his mother must be at her wit's end with him, she thought.

"It seems ye have a way with the wee bairns, Lady Abigale." Marcus stood next to her leaning a shoulder against the stone wall.

"Aye." She smiled and stood up. "They are precious, a true gift from God." Her eyes followed Niven as he took off towards the kitchen. Abigale shook her head and laughed. "That lad has a head full of rocks."

Marcus smirked. "Highlanders tend to have a stubborn streak."

Abigale was beginning to find his statement true.

"Seeing yer mother murdered right before yer eyes will scar ye for life."

Stunned, Abigale turned and faced Marcus. "He saw his mother die?"

"Aye. We believe he was only five summers old when it happened. 'Tis a shame. James allowed the boy to stay here. In fact, the lad has grown quite fond of yer husband and has become one of the stable grooms. Clumsy, but he cares for the horses quite well."

"How old is he?"

"Ten-and-two, we believe."

"Thank God James had given the lad a home. I can't imagine what he has been through." Abigale searched the hall until James came into view. He was with his men, talking. As she watched him from across the room, it warmed her heart knowing what James had done. He'd saved Niven's life. The Bogeyman didn't seem so evil after all, she pondered.

The tempo of the music picked up to a jig as a tin whistle joined the harp. A few ladies danced to the music while the men drank their mead and recalled a time in their younger years when they could keep up with the lassies.

Abigale noticed Magnus as he stood and readjusted his tunic over his plump belly. He searched through the great hall as if looking for someone. "Och Alice, you bonny lass, come dance with me!" he yelled out over the crowded tables.

Alice stood with her hands on her hips and said, "I thought ye'd never ask."

As they joined in with the other dancers in front of the great hall, Abigale watched them as Magnus twirled Alice to the music. She sighed. She wished that that was her and James dancing to the music. Holding her close, feeling his strong body next to hers, all the while making her feel as if she was the only lass in the room. She sighed again. *Oh, what a wonderful feeling that must be*, she thought. *Abigale Bruce, even if he asked ye to dance there's one small problem. Ye don't know how to dance.*

Looking away from the dancing couples in disappointment, she began to leave the sitting area when Marcus grabbed her arm. "Lady Abigale, would ye care to dance?"

Oh no! Was she that readable… was she that pathetic that he was going to show her mercy by asking her to dance? Quickly Abigale thought of an excuse. "Thank ye kindly, but I dinnae think my husband would take kindly to me dancing with another man."

Marcus pulled her closer to him. "James is my cousin. 'Tis fine."

"Aye, how silly of me to have forgotten." How was she going to get out of this situation? For certain she would look like a fool stumbling and stomping all over his feet. A princess was expected to be a graceful dancer, for that's how you caught the eye of an admirer. At least that was what she was told; there was no dancing allowed at the nunnery. Oh, she could just hear the laughter now throughout the hall as their graceless princess fell straight on her arse.

"Come." Marcus nodded to the couples dancing and started to guide her toward them.

Abigale planted her feet on the ground and tried to pull away from his grip. "Nay. I cannae."

Confusion swept Marcus's face. "Why not? I told ye, James won't mind," he reassured her.

There was no telling this man no. True to his word, Highlanders were stubborn men. In order to save herself from the humiliation, she had to tell him the truth. Taking in a deep breath and then slowly letting it go, she dropped her gaze to the floor. "I dinnae know how to dance," Abigale closed her eyes, anticipating his laughter.

Marcus placed his finger under her chin tipping her head up. "Och Lady Abigale, ye're in good hands I can assure ye. I'd be honored to teach ye."

Abigale shyly smiled. "Are ye sure?"

He placed his hand over his chest. "On my honor."

Marcus took her by the arm and led her in front of the great hall where they joined the other dancers. Placing her right hand into his, he spun Abigale around as if he was showing off a prized possession. Pulling her close, he smiled. "Relax, follow my lead."

Marcus was quite a gentleman, he never once complained when Abigale stepped on his foot or tripped over her own. They just laughed about it and continued their dance. He spun her with grace and she truly felt beautiful. Abigale was surprised how quickly she caught on and by the third dance she was the one who led.

When the dance ended, she was winded and her cheeks hurt from smiling so much. Marcus was indeed a skillful dancer and an excellent instructor. Leading them over to a table so Abigale could sit and regain her breath, Marcus poured her a drink, and sat across the table from her. He leaned over it as if he had a secret to tell. "May I speak openly, my lady?"

"Of course, ye shall." Curious to what he had to say, she leaned in closer.

"My cousin is a fool for allowing his bonny wife to dance with another man. If ye were my wife I'd never allow it."

The intensity of his statement left Abigale uneasy. Certainly, she had enjoyed dancing with Marcus and adored his company, but she hoped that she didn't give him the wrong impression. "I must go. Thank ye for the dance." Without causing a scene, she quickly excused herself.

~~~~~

Long, sharp talons protruded from James's fingertips and scored the wooden table top. The more he watched Marcus twirl Abigale around as they danced, the deeper his daggers plunged into the wood. Marcus was mocking him, wasn't he? Pulling her body close, feeling her soft curves. The bastard knew exactly what he was doing. James growled profoundly.

This foreign sensation of uncontrolled jealousy surged through him. It cranked his dragon senses to hyper-sensitive. Never had he felt this way before and quite frankly he didn't like it.

James raked his claws down the table leaving a trail of splintered wood behind as he saw Marcus whisper into Abigale's ear. His focus stayed on Abigale the whole time. God's bones! The urge to jump over the table and rip Marcus's head from his body was consuming every fiber in his body. His dragon vibrated and rumbled inside of him and itched to be released.

The sound of wood cracking caught Conall's attention. A sharp pain blasted across James's shin as Conall kicked him. Snapping his head up, he shot his best friend a lethal look.

Wide-eyed, Conall tipped his chin to James's claws.

As James looked down, shiny black talons stared back at him. Instantly he retracted them.

Shite, what the hell was wrong with him? Never had he lost control like that, not in public. This was not the place nor time to be testing his dragon's appetite for blood. Rubbing the back of his neck, he blew out a heavy sigh. He grabbed his tankard and drained it dry.

"Are ye alright?" Conall asked.

"Aye." James took out his frustrations on his tankard as he slammed it down onto the table. "Need more mead."

~~~~~

As Abigale weaved through the crowded great hall, she was stopped a few times to be introduced to clan members. Names and faces started to blur, for she had met so many people in such a short amount of time, it made her head hurt. Furthermore, her feet were killing her. All she wanted to do was to slip into bed and drift off to sleep.

As she reached the stairs leading to her bedchamber, she paused. The hairs on the nape of her neck started to stand and her body warmed as amber eyes penetrated her skin. Her cheeks blushed pink as a wave of nervousness ran through her, making her palms sweat. No need to confirm; James was watching her, watching her every move.

Abigale was relieved when she finally reached her bedchamber. She hurried out of her dress, changed into a clean shift, and now stood by a window that looked out over the rolling moonlit hills. Beyond the hills lay a grey shadow of a mountain range that disappeared into the night sky. Soon their peaks would be powdered with snow. Combing through a wave of auburn hair, she thought that would be a wonderful place to take Fergus for a ride.

The wooden door to her bedchamber slammed open. Two huge dogs barreled through and leapt onto the bed, making themselves right at home. Startled, Abigale raced to the bed. "Ye smelly mongrels, get down… shoo!" A wet tongue lapped at her face while the other dog made himself comfortable at the end of the bed.

"Sorry lass, Lennox and Mahboon stay." James filled the door frame as he staggered pulling his boots off.

"What are ye doing here?" This was her bedchamber, so she thought. It was the same room she had been in last night.

"This is my bedchamber, Abigale. I should be asking ye the same question." James pulled his tunic up over his head and started to fumble with his kilt.

Holy Mary, Mother of God. He was undressing right before her eyes. She had never seen a man naked before. Well, that was not completely true. Did her patients in the infirmary count? Nay, no one came close to the man standing before her. Her first response was to close her eyes and look away, but female instincts told her to gaze upon every corded muscle the man was offering. Her eyes gazed upon his tanned, muscled chest to the ripples of his abdomen to the line of fine dark hair that disappeared below his plaid.

"This is what ye want… no?" James asked.

Abigale snapped her head up to find James in pursuit, stalking her like she was his prey. For every dominating step forward he took, she took two steps back in retreat until the coldness of the stone wall bit into her back and she was trapped, pinned to the wall by his body. He pressed against her. Instantly she felt his heat radiate through the light material of her shift. Her heart quickened in anticipation. Fluttering tingles filled her core and her breasts ached for his touch. God help her, she wanted this man.

Abigale felt his arm move and prayed he was going to touch her, but instead he rested his forearm on the stone wall above her head. He brushed his lips down to her lower neck. With one long flick of his tongue he licked her all the way up to the soft spot just below her ear as if he was tasting her. "Ye have my attention, lass. Now what are ye going to do with it?"

The slick softness of his tongue sent tingles throughout her body and her legs threatened to buckle. Breathing became difficult as her chest worked hard to pump air through her lungs. *Well Abigale, what are ye going to do?* A gorgeously naked man stood before her. A man who claimed he did not want her, yet here he was encaging her with his massive frame. Was this his way of intimidating her, to scare her, and make her leave the bedchamber? Intimidation did not set well with her; in fact it brought out her feisty side. No more would she allow threats to rule her life like they had back at the nunnery. Should she dare call his bluff and make the first move? Mayhap he wasn't bluffing at all, she thought. Instincts told her to tread cautiously, but her body craved his touch. Something about the way he made her feel brought out her bravery and she was going to claim her first kiss.

Never having been kissed before, she didn't know where to start. Should she place her hands on his shoulders or should she wrap her arms around his waist? Should she close her eyes or leave them open? Awkward didn't begin to describe how she was feeling right now. Wasn't the man supposed to make the first move? *Not if they are all as stubborn as James Douglas,* she thought.

She placed her hands on his chest. Aye, this felt right. Astonished by the sinew of his muscles, her fingers explored his smooth chest. All the while James nibbled up and down her neck. Her thumb grazed over his nipple causing him to growl deeply. So, she did have an effect on him after all. She smiled to herself.

Abigale snaked her arms around his neck and pulled his head closer to hers. The ampleness of his lips enticed her, she needed to taste him. Without hesitation she licked his bottom lip and drew its fullness into her mouth. To her surprise, he opened his mouth, inviting her in, and allowing her to take control. As she guided her tongue into his mouth, she felt its warmness and could smell the mead on his breath. Passion drove her forward and she deepened the kiss until she felt weightless.

The kiss ended too quickly as James pulled away. "Och, if I'm not to yer liking I can go find Marcus."

"Marcus?" In one moment she had been consumed by this magical kiss, and all the while James had been concerned about Marcus. Did he really think that she wanted to bed another man? It was just a dance, nothing more.

James's eyes pinned her deep blues, "Ye didnae seem to mind his company earlier."

"I only danced with him because he's yer cousin." Abigale tried to reassure him, but it seemed he didn't believe her.

"I have an idea… I'll go fetch Marcus and he can join us. What say ye?" James started to pull up her shift.

"Enough, ye're drunk." Abigale swatted at his chest. "There's no need to be jealous. It was just a dance."

"Jealous?" James released his grip on her shift. "Nay, I care not." He walked away from her and made his way to the bed. His massive naked body sprawled out over black furs while Lennox and Mahboon took up residence at the foot of the bed. James folded his hands behind his head nonchalantly. "Last offer, lass. Aye or nay."

Most definitely nay, he was drunk and wanted to claim her out of pure jealousy. Damn him and his stubborn egotistical ways. Abigale stormed over to the bed and grabbed a fur. "I'd rather sleep in a byre."

"Suit yerself, but if ye change yer mind-"

"Ye're a barbaric arse." And with that said, Abigale quit the bedchamber.

Chapter 8

Confessed faults are half-mended. ~ *Scottish Proverb*

James woke to a wet kiss on his cheek and heavy panting in his ear. He swatted at the annoying noise and moaned in protest. Another kiss and James cracked open an eye and there in his peripheral vision sat Lennox, his prized hunting dog, staring at him and panting. "Enough, lassie." James wiped the slobber from his cheek and sat up. His stomach lurched, the room spun, and he grabbed his head as if it would help stop it from spinning out of control. Dazed amber eyes searched the bedchamber for any sign of life, but no one was there except his dogs. Closing his eyes he sent a grateful plea to the Gods that be that he was alone. God's teeth, mead was going to be the death of him.

As James lay back down, he was surprised he had fallen asleep. Nightmares of death usually haunted his dreams; therefore peaceful slumber eluded him most of the time. Unless the amber liquid went down smooth, then it never failed, he would drink until the mead took over. Normally a lass would be lurking around willing and ready to please. It helped pass the time until dawn.

A vision of Abigale dancing with Marcus invaded his thoughts as he recalled the way her dress flowed to the music. Her body twirled and swayed with grace and beauty like nothing he had ever seen before. For a moment he was content just watching her from across the great hall. Her face softened with a smile and the sound of her laughter soothed his soul.

That was until he had noticed the way Marcus had set his wandering eyes on her. Just like a snake in the Garden of Eden, Marcus was testing his limits, waiting to strike, and make his move. Aye, he did not trust him for one moment, and that's when the drinking began. *James Douglas, if ye were half the man ye thought ye were, ye would have claimed that dance last night instead of letting another man invade yer claim.* Aye, if only he was just a man, mayhap he could be the one for Abigale.

James licked his lips and swallowed hard, still tasting Abigale's kiss that lingered on the tip of his tongue like it had just happened. *Shite.* He had been such an arse to her. He had tried to walk past her bedchamber last eve, but his body betrayed him. After seeing another man up close and personal with Abigale it took all his strength not to throw her on the bed and take her... brand her... sear her body with his, so every Dragonkine or man would know she belonged to him. But he could not do it, so he took the coward's way out by intimidating her. His eyes flew open. *Abigale?* She was here. He leaned over and felt the sheets next to him; they were cold.

James sat up, pulled his hands through his hair, and Lennox hopped off the bed. "Och lassie, 'tis time to lick my wounds and go find Lady Abigale." Lennox ran to the door, Mahboon right behind her, they both scratched at it. Donning his kilt and tunic, he quit the bedchamber.

The last place James looked for Abigale was in the horse stable, knowing all along she would be here, yet he didn't want to face the consequences of last night's blunder. The sweet smell of fresh cut hay filled the stone framed room. Chargers of white, black, and chestnut were lined up on one side of the wall standing side by side only separated by wooden walls. They paid James no mind as he walked down the main aisle. As he approached the next stall a black mare nickered. James patted her on her hindquarters. "Settle lass, 'tis me," he whispered.

Passing an empty stall he thought mayhap Abigale wasn't here. He began to turn around and leave until he heard a soft sigh and the crunch of hay. *Abigale?*

Curled up in a fur on a hay pallet next to Fergus, Abigale slept. A soft gray muzzle was buried in her auburn hair next to her flawless face as if the steed was protecting a prized possession. Long, black eyelashes rested on her cheeks that were pink from the cold night air. Her lips quivered. God's blood, he was an arse.

As James got closer, Fergus stirred and pinned his ears back, telling James to proceed with caution. "Easy lad." James's voice was a mere whisper. "I will no hurt her." He held out his hand and Fergus nipped at it. Retracting his hand quickly, James took a step back. *Easy, two steps forward one step back.* Fergus stood as to not wake Abigale and pinned his ears again. James held his hands up in surrender. "I know… I know… I messed up. Let me take her inside to get warm." This was a first, he thought, negotiating with a horse.

Fergus raised his head to intimidate James, then neighed a deep confident nicker. James reached, down never losing eye contact with the stallion and grabbed a hand full of hay. He offered it to Fergus. "See lad, I'm not so bad, am I?" The protective warhorse paused. Slowly with caution he lowered his head and blew out a puff of hot air from his nostrils like he was calming his nerves. With his neck stretched out he investigated the peace offering by moving the hay around with his nose. James took his other hand and stroked Fergus's pure white forehead. "Peace?"

Finally, after three handfuls of hay and a promised carrot or two, Fergus deemed James as a friend for now, and allowed passage to Abigale. He went down on bended knee beside her. Peaceful like a child she slept. Gently, he took her in his strong arms, and Abigale snuggled deep into his warmth. She felt perfect against his chest, almost like she was made for him. He thought himself a hundred times a fool for being rough with her… intimidating her. The oath he had taken was to protect her and aye, he could do that, but could he protect her from himself?

James entered his bedchamber and laid Abigale down on a warm bed billowing with furs and pillows. "James?" Abigale said, half asleep, half awake.

"Shhh my *bel ange*. Rest." He placed his hand on her forehead as his magic washed over her sending her into a restful sleep. He tucked the blankets snug around her body and kissed her forehead. Before he left the room he placed more peat on the fire. The lass had to go.

The next morn before the sun rose over the village indicating a new day had come, James and his men left on a long hunting jaunt. He needed to clear his thoughts, take in some cool Highland air, bond with his Dragonkine brethren while hunting red deer and boar. He needed to refocus on recruiting neighboring clans to join clan Douglas and fight for the king. This was not an easy task at hand, for Scotland was unstable and fragmented. Kinsmen fought kinsmen over who they thought should be the rightful king of Scotland. Ally with the wrong clan and truces would be broken between allies. James had seen clans wiped out, completely slaughtered, just because they joined forces with accused traitors.

Even though King Robert took him off the battlefield to protect his daughter, it didn't mean he couldn't aid in the king's rebellion against England. He would always do what he had to do to rid Scotland of the English. Furthermore, there was always a battle to be fought and he would be prepared when the time came.

James led the way north toward the Great Glen. Mounted upon his black mare, James looked very much the natural born leader he was. The black mare was massive, unusual for a female warhorse, but she was just as dominant as James. James and Conall took the dirt path deeper into the glen, while Rory and Magnus followed the trail to the loch. A flawless strategy was set in motion to draw out the hunt, surround the prey, and then go in for the kill.

James sensed that Conall needed to get something off his chest. Both men side by side walked their fine steeds at a steady pace along the forest path keeping their eyes alert, searching the thick vegetation for clues of deer.

"Abigale seems to be a fine lass," Conall said.

James adjusted himself in his saddle. "Aye. Alice is verra fond of her."

"Ye know James, it might not be all that bad to have a wife… warming yer bed every night." Conall dared a glance at James, arched a black brow, and grinned.

"Conall, you can stop right there… I know what ye are doing. I took a vow to protect King Robert's daughter and that I intend to do, for he has been nothing less than a father to me. I owe him for helping me get my lands back. I didnae ask for her to be my wife, nor do I want her as my wife." For Christ sake, was he ever going to escape the lass?

Halting their horses, Conall tried to reason with James. "But, ye have a wife, a verra beautiful one."

James shot him a hard stern glare warning his friend to tread softly. "Did ye forget? We are Dragonkine, Conall! How do I explain this to her!" James pointed to his eyes as they turned to a swirling amber with reptilian slits.

"Och—"

"Nay, I'm sending her to Bothwell Castle and that's final!" James kicked his horse forward, ending their conversation. The more Conall brought up Abigale the more aggravated he became. After he left his bedchamber last night he pondered ways to solve his problem, and sending Abigale to Bothwell was the best plan of attack. They could still go on as husband and wife, but would live separate lives. She would be close enough to protect, yet far away from him. 'Twas a plan he was sure Abigale would be fond of, for she would be able to keep part of her dowry and he could keep his honor with the king.

He was letting her go… sending her away. The realization hit his heart like the muscle was being squeezed by a steel plated gauntlet. He felt the coldness of the steel bite deeper into his lifeline. The restraint intensified leaving him aching. James rubbed the pain in his chest as he felt his dragon mourn their loss.

"James, listen to me."

James shook off his thoughts. It was apparent he had to listen to Conall because his best friend wasn't taking no for an answer. God's teeth, Conall could be a persistent nag.

"Think of it like this... like a battle. Ye go to battle to fight for what's right. 'Tis a long hard battle, ye dinnae like it, but ye know at the end there will be peace. A woman is no different. Ye fight for her love, ye dinnae like the feelings she brings out of ye at first, but my friend, if she's the one, trust in me when I say to let go and ye'll find there's nothing like a woman's love to soothe yer dragon side."

James mused for a moment. Had his friend gone daft? How could a ruthless, bloodthirsty dragon bring anyone peace? Nonetheless, how can ye bring peace when ye're no at ease with yerself?

"Conall, are ye daft? Did ye leave yer ballocks back home?"

It looked as if a huge boulder crashed down on Conall. "Rest assured my Laird, my balls are just fine. I thank ye for yer concern." Conall nodded his head and trotted his horse toward the sandy trail leading to the loch. There was no getting past that thick skull.

James let out a heavy exhalation and continued through the glen, finally alone with his own thoughts. Hellfire, his blood burned in irritation. His best friend... talking about love and women... he had to have been bewitched. Conall Hamilton hadn't fallen under a lass's spell... had he? "Nay."

The squawk of a flock of black birds fleeing from a thicket of blackthorns on top of a hill caught James's attention. He watched the birds as they scattered like black specks littering the sky. There was no time to move or even flee as James saw an arrow fly through the air from the thicket and plunge into his heart with precise aim.

~~~~~

Victoria Zak

A wise man once said that patience was not a virtue, but a vice. A wicked moral, testing the true heart of a man. When fortitude was tested, it separated the weak from the strong, the faithful from the faithless. He knew this all to be true, he lived it every day. Now as fate would have it he would seek out what was rightfully his and gain its benefits. Not only did he have to possess patience, but he had to know when to strike and to push a little harder to achieve his goals. Perched high on top of a green mounding hill hidden behind a thicket of dense blackthorns, he waited for his glory. If fate would allow, the Gods would bless him this day.

He reached behind him and pulled out a long shaft from the leather quiver on his back. As he sat there fondling the feather-light flight, his thoughts of being on the battlefield came to mind. James on bended knee being knighted by the king of Scotland, a banner in his honor, and the king's daughter as a reward. It should have been him on bended knee being honored, not James. He should be the one with a banner in his name with men aplenty behind him. His blood had been shed on the battlefield that day. Shouldn't he reap the benefits of land and a pretty princess to warm his bed? All of his life he had been second to James, but not today. He would outwit the clan's chief, uproot the house of Douglas, and become a legend... the man who slayed the Bogeyman.

Dull green leaves turning to a pale yellow thinly littered the blackthorn bushes. The blue-black color of the berries on its branches beckoned him to reach up and pick a berry. He studied it for a moment before placing it in his mouth. A bitter taste shot through his mouth reminding him winter was on its way. *After first freeze the berries would taste much sweeter,* he thought.

After he spat out the remainder of the sour berry, he walked over to the spot that would give him the best vantage point. Looking down upon the trail, he knew it wouldn't be long; his target would be approaching soon. He felt in his bones that his time was now. He grabbed his longbow that was resting by an autumn-stricken tree and paused for a moment. As he looked at the black contorted skeleton of a blackthorn tree it mocked him, revealing how twisted and evil his soul had become.

Jealousy throughout the years had weaved through him and cloaked his heart in blackness. *Ye are the keeper of dark secrets, lad,* the tree mocked again. It was going to be a blackthorn winter, he thought with a smirk.

To him, a traitor was nothing more than an actor upon the stage only revealing what seems fit at the moment. A master of lies and deception, he had played his part well throughout the years. Just like patience, betrayal had become second nature. A coat of many colors he wore, but his purpose stayed true. Friend or foe, ally or enemy, he waited to make his move, showing no mercy upon the fools who stood in his way.

Much more than retaliation for his misfortunes was on the line. He fought for someone more precious to him than the air he breathed. An innocent victim handpicked and strategically placed on the game board to be played by someone else for their gains. Nay, there was no turning back.

Feet planted true and firm like the excellent archer he was, he raised his bow, and notched the shaft. He surveyed the trail once more as he drew back the poisoned arrow. Feathers lightly brushed his neatly trimmed jawline, reminding him of how sweet Abigale's kisses would be and how sweet victory would taste. *Soon my pet, verra soon.*

All thoughts pushed aside, he took aim and released the string, sending the arrow straight to his target. James's heart.

Chapter 9

Were it not for hope the heart would break. ~ *Scottish Proverb*

A powerful force knocked James from his horse. He landed firmly on his back on the hard forest floor. Air rushed out of his lungs and his torso stung as he clamped a hand over the sting to relieve the pain. As he looked at his chest, a red circle crept across his tunic. In the middle of that blood-soaked spot, an arrow shot in perfect accuracy plunged deep into his skin. He had been a target, indeed his heart marked the spot.

The smell of dirt and blood invaded his senses. He rolled back and forth and arched in pain, but there was no escaping the blazing heat burning through his veins like fire. Confusion hit him hard; one strike from an arrow shouldn't have caused him this much pain, after all he was immortal. Even after a fatal blow he could fight off death and regain his strength, but this was different. The pain was agony, the blood poured rapidly from his body, and his strength weakened. With his throat dry and swollen, a mere grunt was all James had left in him as he tried to yell for help.

Darkness was closing in. As he drifted, a vision of Abigale floating in the loch flashed before him. Long auburn hair splayed out around her flawless face, a thin wet shift clung to every curve as the water licked at her delectable body. James remembered how he itched to run his hands over her breasts, feel the hardness of her pebbled peaks, and taste her sweetness. Her body beckoned to be touched. Now it was too late... too late to tell her what a fool he had been... too late to claim her.

~~~~~

At the first crack of light, Abigale was up and ready for the day. She had planned to keep herself busy and rid herself of all thoughts of a certain Highlander. First thing this morn, she had helped in the kitchen preparing the vegetables for the night's feast and staying clear of anything that involved fire. By noon she had crushed some lavender into a mixture to bathe the smelly dogs. If the hounds from hell were going to be regular visitors in her bedchamber they had to be bathed, for they smelled like a dung heap. As she crumpled the sweet-smelling lavender into a bowl, a little harder than needed, she vowed a few times to hate James Douglas for as long as she lived, especially after last eve's kiss. It was a good thing he was nowhere in sight, because undoubtedly he would have received the sharp end of her tongue. "Barbarian," she thought out loud.

After the challenging experience of bathing Lennox and Mahboon, Abigale made her way into the solar where Alice and Effie sat by the hearth working on their embroidery. Abigale walked in and plopped herself down in a chair with a huff.

Concern creased Alice's brows. "What be the worry, lassie?"

Effie spoke up before Abigale could respond, "Didn't yer night go well with Laird Douglas?"

"Effie!" Alice scolded.

"Nay Alice, 'tis alright," Abigale reassured. It was obvious her friends had been worried about her. In fact she hadn't said a word to them all day. "Nothing happened, I assure ye." She crossed her arms and blew out a hard breath. "James had too much mead and blacked out." Purposely, she'd left out the small, yet mortifying detail of how foolish she'd felt kissing him and being turned away. No need to mark herself a total fool.

Alice snorted and held back a laugh.

"Alice, do no laugh, Abigale is devastated." Effie jumped out of her chair, rushed over to Abigale, and embraced her with a sympathetic hug.

"Effie, I appreciate yer concern, but I'm more mad than devastated. When we first met he told me he didnae want me as a wife. I guess... I mean... I just thought maybe one kiss and he would change his mind."

Abigale shrugged her shoulders and plucked at the hem of her apron. Looking up sheepishly she revealed, "I spent the night in the stables with Fergus."

All of a sudden the women broke out in laughter. Abigale joined their laughter, for she had to laugh. Frankly she was too flustered by James's behavior to break down and cry. How could James be jealous of another man when he had no feelings for her? Why should he care who she danced with or chose to talk to? It didn't make sense to her.

Alice set her embroidery down and shook her head. "Highlanders. They're so damn stubborn." She turned to face Abigale. "Dear Lady Abigale, he's trying to push ye away because he likes ye and he does no like how it is making him feel."

"Oh Alice, I do wish it to be true, but he has made it clear as to where I stand."

"Nonsense lass, ye are a beautiful woman… a princess of Scotland… he should be so lucky to be wanted by ye."

Abigale huffed and blew a strand of hair from her eyes. James brought out Abigale's curiosity; that was for certain. She wanted to know how it would feel to be loved by a beautiful, intimidating Highlander. After seeing him naked and tasting his kisses, she hungered to explore every muscled inch of his body, to run her fingers through his wavy locks, but most of all she yearned to be wanted by this man. She didn't know why she felt like this. Mayhap it was his masculinity; the way she felt her body heat when he looked at her or was it the fluttering sensation she felt in her stomach every time he was near? Whatever it may be it was most definitely lust.

Alice held Abigale's hands and sincerely looked into her eyes. "Sometimes a man needs a little push in order to see what he really wants and frankly, I've seen it in his eyes. He likes ye, lass. Laird Douglas might no show it but he does."

"So, what am I to do then? That man is driving me daft."

"Ye seduce him." Effie casually stated this fact as if she had done this type of thing before.

Abigale's eyes grew vast with shock. "Seduce him?"

Effie stood up from her chair, unlaced the front of her dress just enough so her breasts teased. She uncoiled her red hair from its bun and flicked it free. "This is how it's done." Effie sauntered seductively over to Abigale.

Abigale could feel her cheeks blush in embarrassment. What was Effie up to?

The redhead placed a hand on the back of Abigale's chair and leaned forward until the tops of her breasts bulged from her dress. With her free hand she playfully rubbed her neck and trailed her fingertips down toward her chest. "My Laird, do ye see anything ye like?" she purred.

Abigale's cheeks turned three shades of red. She playfully pushed Effie away and started to giggle.

"Effie!" Alice reprimanded with shock.

"What?" Effie stood up and shrugged her shoulders. "If she wants to get the laird's attention she must have some tricks up her sleeve."

Abigale tried to stop laughing. She could see why the men took a liking to Effie. Unlike herself, Effie was confident, beautiful, and bold. If only she could be as bold. Finally she caught her breath. "I'm afraid, lassies, no matter how much I show my bits, the laird does no desire me."

Alice picked up her needlework and tugged a needle through the fabric with a sly grin. "Rubbish," she harrumphed. "The laird watches ye like he wants to tear yer dress off yer body. Dinnae worry aboot a thing."

Abigale's mood started to lighten. It felt good to talk freely with Alice and Effie. This must be how it felt to have a sister; someone to jest with, someone to confide in, someone to love unconditionally. Sure the sisters at the abbey were friendly, but this was different. Without judgment or punishment, she could be herself.

Thunderous footsteps and loud boisterous voices rang throughout the great hall in panic, sending the women to their feet. They rushed to the hall to see what the ruckus was about. The scene Abigale saw taking place right in front of her scared her more than being captured by the English. Conall held a bloody, lifeless body in his arms. With haste, she hurried over to Conall. "Blessed Mary!" Abigale's hand flew over her mouth in horror. "James?"

Conall pushed past Abigale. "Alice, fetch the healer," he roared. "He's been shot with an arrow in the chest."

"Wait, I can help," Abigale pleaded.

"We dinnae have time to spare, my lady. Our chief needs the healer."

Blood poured continuously from his chest and splattered on to the stone floor. Abigale's instincts jolted to life as she took over.

"Conall, take James to his bedchamber and Alice, bring me blankets, lots of them. Effie boil some water." Abigale began to make her way to the stairs, but when she looked back Conall still stood where he was. "Conall Hamilton if ye dinnae move yer arse I'll see it hung!"

Taken aback by her sternness Conall shot up the stairs, taking them two at a time.

James's bloodied body lay on the bed. Abigale started to rip his tunic off and examine the extent of his wounds. "How did this happen?"

"My lady, we were out hunting… we split up… and…" Conall rubbed his hand through his hair and started to pace a trench in the floor beside the bed. "He was shot with an arrow. I had to snap it off at the head so that it wouldn't go deeper." He pointed at the blood rushing out of James's chest.

In all her time at the nunnery's infirmary mending wounds she had never seen a man survive with this much blood loss. "We need to stop the bleeding."

Alice came bolting through the door with an arm full of blankets. Abigale grabbed a small cloth and blotted the blood away from the wounded area. If only she could stop the bleeding long enough, she might be able to find the arrowhead.

Lifting the blood-soaked cloth, she saw an inch of the shaft poking through his flesh. "Alice, go into the top drawer of my nightstand. There's a satchel... in that satchel you'll find a reddish-purple flower... I need it worked into a paste with boiling hot water. Can ye do that for me?"

"Aye, my lady." Before Abigale could finish her request, Alice had already rushed out of the chamber with the purple flower in her hand.

"James." Abigale touched his face and he moaned in pain. "I have to remove the arrow... bite down on this." Abigale placed a rolled up cloth in James's mouth and motioned for Conall to assist her.

"Rory... Marcus... hold his body down. Magnus, give me your whiskey." Abigale took the whiskey and poured it over the wound which caused James to arch in tremendous pain. "Sorry," Abigale winced.

As the whiskey washed away the pooling blood, Abigale had a good view of the wooden shaft. Thank God, the head had not punctured his heart. Gently she pulled on the shaft, testing how deep its barbs had set in. "The head is stuck." Abigale turned to the men. "Do ye have an arrow spoon... an arrow puller?"

The men looked at her like she had gone daft. Arrow spoon?

Abigale took that as a nay. Continuing to blot away at the blood, she noticed that there was more of the arrowhead showing than before. *Unbelievable,* she thought. She paused and observed James's wound closer. *'Tis like his body is pushing the arrow out from his chest.*

Gently, Abigale wrapped her hand around the arrowhead and maneuvered it out of his chest, causing James to jerk with such force that his arm slipped free and threatened to hit Abigale. Rory strained to gain control again. "Sorry... my lady," he grunted, "'Tis like trying to hold down a hogget during a shearing."

As the blood rushed over her hands, Abigale didn't have much time to think. She needed to seal up her husband's wound, but which plan of action should she take? If she used a hot poker the pain alone could kill him or she could place her faith in healing herbs. One wrong decision and she could be a widow.

Alice rushed in with a wooden bowl. "My lady." She offered the paste to Abigale. The healing herbs would have to work, for she didn't know how much more pain her husband could endure. Quickly she began to smear the purple concoction around and inside the wound. "This will help stop the bleeding and dull his pain. We are going to need to lift him. I need to wrap a pressure bandage around his chest," Abigale instructed.

Abigale kept the rags snug against the wound while the men lifted James to a sitting position. James's head fell back and his eyes rolled to the back of his head. Sweet Jesus, it was going to take a miracle to save this man.

"Effie, hold pressure here." Abigale took Effie's hands and placed them firmly on the wound. "Alice, help me wrap his chest."

After they wrapped the laird's chest, they laid him back down on to the bed. Abigale stood over James. He was pale and his breathing was slow, but steady. Sending a prayer up to heaven, she prayed that her healing skills would help her husband and bring him back to her. She couldn't lose him, not now… not ever.

Abigale's nerves lay bare. Raw emotions from the severity of James's condition threatened to take her over. She must not fall apart now. *Abigale Bruce get it together*, she scolded herself. Taking a deep breath she walked over and grabbed the wash basin. Trying desperately to keep calm, Abigale began to wash the bloodstains from his body. Sweat glistened over his unconscious body and it felt as if it was on fire. If the blood loss didn't kill him, the fever would.

As Abigale peered up from wiping a smear of blood from James's forearm, she saw his kinsmen standing around the bed grief-stricken as they looked down upon their fallen chief. These men had so much respect for their ruthless leader. If she was the betting type, she would have bet that anyone of them would have traded places with him and taken the blow of that blasted arrow.

Alice placed a hand on Abigale's shoulder and reached for the wash rags. "Let me. Ye should get some rest." She nodded her head in James's direction, "He's in God's hands now."

"Nay!" Abigale shook her head and snatched the rag away from Alice. "I will no leave his side."

Abigale didn't mean to be so rude, but the thought of leaving James made her heart stop beating and her lungs deflate. What if he awoke and she wasn't there? What if he was in pain or what if he started to bleed again? No, she had to be right here by his side.

Magnus cleared his throat. "My lady." He wiped a fallen tear nonchalantly from his cheek. "Is there anything else we can do?"

"Aye," Abigale choked out a faint whisper, "Go to the chapel and pray."

As the last man quit the room, Abigale rubbed her face against James's hand. "James Douglas, this is no time for ye to be stubborn." She sniffed and fought back tears. "Come back to me." Her vision clouded, her hands began to tremble, and the air thickened, making it difficult for her to breathe. She needed to be close to him, to feel him breathe, and to hear his heartbeat. Without disturbing him, she climbed into bed, laid her head on his chest away from his wound, and sobbed until she fell asleep.

Chapter 10

A debt is owed, the price; his soul.

The sun shone down through the trees casting an amber hue throughout the glen. "James." The sweetness of a beautiful voice echoed throughout the forest, warming his skin like sun rays. The soft whisper led James deeper into the glen. As he searched for the sound, a glimpse of a sheer dress hem wisped around a tree slowly and disappeared behind it. "James." There it was again, washing over his skin like warm honey from the comb. His body ached to feel its warmth. "Come back to me." He tracked the enchanting sound behind the tree, but to his disappointment, nothing was there. *Where was the voice coming from?*

The wind brushed over fallen leaves sending them whirling around James's feet. The hairs on the back of his neck rose, his body tensed, and his curiosity ran wild. With caution, he turned his large body around and couldn't believe his eyes.

"Abigale?"

Wearing a sheer white long-sleeved gown, Abigale stood in front of him. Her long auburn hair floated through the wind, engulfing him with her sweet scent. He reached out to touch her. She was so close, yet too far away. "Abigale," James whispered.

Her beauty shone through the sun rays as she stepped into James's embrace. He held her tight, feeling every lush curve of her body. Running his hands through her hair, he confirmed that she was really here. Well, at least she felt real, but this had to be a dream. In disbelief, James took a step back and looked her up and down. "What are ye doing here, lass?"

Abigale gently stroked his face and stared deeply into his smoldering depths. "Come back to me, James. I need ye."

Aye, definitely this was a sweet dream.

All of a sudden the forest grew dead silent and darkness closed in around them. Panic-stricken, James grabbed Abigale's arms a little too firmly. "Abigale, ye must leave. He's coming for me."

"Nay, come with me, please," Abigale begged.

Off in the distance James heard a hollow clanking sound echoing through the glen that seemed to grow closer and approached fast. He looked behind him to see where the noise was coming from. The forest trees moved closer together. Branches touched creating a tunnel, and the dirt trail narrowed into a long endless destination.

James knew who had tracked him down and waited patiently for his soul. This was the reason he didn't sleep at night, for the bloody bastard haunted his every dream. A cruel, twisted game the menace craved to play. Hunting James as if he were prey. He toyed with James's mind night after night with visions of his father's bloody body being tortured, all the while laughing vilely at James's distress.

The soul collector knew no boundaries, he collected at will. James had to get Abigale out of his Hell... now! The bloody bastard could have his damned soul, but not Abigale's. She was everything good and pure in his world, the light to his darkness.

James turned back around to warn Abigale to run, but much to his surprise she was already gone, leaving a trail of light behind. Desperately he wanted to follow her light, to bathe in her warmth. If only he believed in heaven, then most definitely she had been heaven sent... his angel... his *bel ange*.

The air around James cooled. An icy chill slid down his spine, and settled in his bones. He peered down the darkened tunnel, trying to see where the noise was coming from. He felt the ground shake and the smell of sulfur assaulted his nose. "The Essence of Hell."

The atmosphere rippled like a stone thrown into still water. Horse hooves pounded like thunder to the earth as a menace raced with purpose, led by unearthly beasts biting at their bits, glowing eyes, and red foam bubbling from their mouths. Black skulls and bones highlighted in silver covered the horse-drawn coach, grayed femur bones acted as spokes on the four wheels that rolled in unison.

James dove out of the way as the raging team was halted by a black cloaked, faceless coachman. Silver chains connecting the rig to the horses rattled a sinister song as it drew to a complete stop.

James hopped to his feet in battle stance ready for a fight. An eerie creak bounced off the trees as the door to the coach slowly opened. Heavy hooves pawed viciously at the ground, growing impatient. A black chain mail glove appeared from the open door motioning with a thick finger for James to come join him.

This was it, James thought. The collector had finally caught up to him. He had been running from this moment all his life. The moment of truth... payment for the sins he'd committed. The slain would be avenged... wrongs would be righted... his soul was the price.

Tired of avoiding his destiny, he began to walk over to the deathly coach ready to embrace the darkness, when a blast of golden light exploded throughout the glen, blinding everything in sight. The dark horses reared up and raged down the rippling tunnel, sending the blasted coach bucking down the trail behind them. The power behind the explosion sent James to the ground. Blackness clouded his vision and the world fell silent.

Chapter 11

He who wants to be a dragon must eat many little snakes. ~ *Chinese Proverb*

"You fool!" Sheriff Rickert raised his leather whip and released its fury upon the man's bare bloodied back. His tone, deep and sharp, filled the damp dungeon. The slender six-foot man with slicked-back salt and pepper hair stood behind his victim. His face, which was aged by the sun and multiple battle scars, possessed a placid anger.

Sheriff Rickert paced around the bloody body until he was face to face with the man. Grabbing the fool's chin, he bore down into his eyes forcing him to look at him. "You were to bring me the Black Douglas. Alive!" he hissed and shoved the man's head back.

Rickert had been a patient man. However, as of late his patience had been strained, pulled taut, and was about to snap. Seven years was a long time for a man to live with a tarnished reputation without revenge. He'd been made a fool the day James Douglas came back to Scotland to reclaim his lands and the family castle. With their chief dead, the clan had been disturbed, which left Castle Douglas defenseless. Being the easy target that it was, Sheriff Rickert and his heavily armed garrison seized the castle and claimed its land.

Oh, but fate could be a bloody bastard. A vicious attack by James on the garrison left Rickert retreating deep into the forest, running like a scared child to his mother. *Coward,* he thought. Flashes of that terrifying night flickered through the sheriff's memory as he recalled the stench of burning flesh and deafening screams. If he hadn't seen it with his own eyes, he would have believed the devil himself had showed up to fight that day. He barely escaped alive. A cold shiver snaked down his spine; he had seen the beast.

"You've failed me. You do know the punishment, don't you?" His English accent dripped with hatred.

The man stood silent as another crack sliced into his back.

"Must I remind you fool, I have something very valuable and precious to you." Rickert stroked his graying goatee. "Your dear sister is at court, unwed and under my protection."

Sheriff Rickert had held the man's sister in the royal court as a hostage of sorts. He promised the man that no harm would come to her if he obeyed his every request. A request to bring him the Black Douglas.

Rickert fondled the leather strip. "Mayhap I should inform King Edward that it's past time for her to wed," he stated.

The man angrily twisted his head to the sheriff and met his devious stare.

Leaning in close to the fool as if he was telling him a secret, he said, "I wonder what a young Scottish piece of arse would feel like." The sheriff's deep chuckle dared the man to break and lose control.

Giving the sheriff no satisfaction, the man balled up his fists and dug his nails deeper into the palms of his hands.

Rickert enjoyed inflicting pain, a master of manipulation. Blackmail was a game he played well. Once he had his eyes on a prize, there was no turning back. He became obsessed with seeking out the right time and place to unleash years of pent up fury. No longer could he walk among the crowds in his hometown and not be heckled about being defeated by a young Scottish lad. A Highlander at that. He was in favour with the king no more; the king saw him as a failure.

James Douglas was an annoying thistle in his arse that needed to be plucked out and destroyed. With the game pieces waiting to be played, his plan had been put into motion. James Douglas wouldn't know what hit him.

~~~~~

The man lowered his head. His body shook from the last crack of the leather whip, or mayhap it was the rage he fought to keep from surfacing. He had to tell the sheriff about his little secret, it was the only way he could keep his sister safe. His beautiful innocent sister was caught up in a dangerous blackmail scheme. He'd failed to protect her. Once the sheriff had his grip on her and sent her to the royal court, he had to go along with Rickert's plan. If he ever wanted to see his sister again, he must bring him the dragon.

Soon it would be over. *Stick to the plan*, he reminded himself. Sometimes you had to shame your soul in order to help destiny along.

The man squeezed his eyes shut and took a deep breath that stung his lungs. "I can bring ye the one thing that will destroy the Black Douglas," he muttered.

This new-found information pricked Rickert's interest. "Do tell."

The man slowly rose his head and seared a stare of hatred into the sheriff's eyes. "I can bring ye Abigale Bruce… James's wife… the princess of Scotland."

Rickert mused. "Capture the princess, and slay the dragon."

Chapter 12

Sometimes life can be as bitter as dragon tears. ~ *Chinese Proverb*

Two days had passed and James lay motionless, his shallow breaths barely moving the sheets covering him. Nonstop caring for Laird Douglas started to take its toll on Abigale. Sleeping only for small amounts of time and eating only when Alice would bring a trencher up to her, she didn't leave his side. Abigale sat by the foot of the bed diligently working on some embroidery. If James didn't wake soon, before long the castle walls would be covered in tapestries. A knock at the door made Abigale jump. She wasn't expecting visitors.

The door creaked open as Marcus peeked in. "Lady Abigale, may I?"

She shook her head, letting him know that it was alright to enter.

Marcus walked to James's bedside and said, "How is he? Any changes?"

"The bleeding has stopped, but he still sleeps." Abigale stood and placed her needlework down on the chair and walked over to James. She felt his forehead. "He's still feverish." His fever should have broken by now, Abigale pondered.

"My lady, forgive me for being blunt but maybe the time has come."

"Nay Marcus, we still have time." Abigale readjusted the covers over James's body.

Marcus walked over to the head of the bed, looking over James's body. "Ye've done everything possible to save him. We can't let him suffer."

Abigale grew irate with him. How dare he come to her with such a request? She was going to save James and nothing or nobody was going to stop her. Something deep inside of her reassured her that she needed this man to live.

Abigale marched over to Marcus and poked a finger at his chest. "Suffer? Do ye think I would let him suffer?"

Marcus stood silently and allowed her to vent.

"I'll spend every last breath making sure my husband lives. His clan needs him!" She challenged him to disagree with her by putting her hands on her hips.

Sharp eyes stared back at her. "And what aboot ye, Lady Abigale? Ye need him too."

Of course she needed James to live. His clan needed him. Being completely honest with herself she needed him too. She couldn't quite put her finger on it, but as soon as he would leave a room she missed him. Furthermore, this was her home and he was her husband. He had to live.

Through shaky breaths and deep sobs, Abigale held on tight and released all her fears on to Marcus's shoulders. "What if Marcus, what if…" She couldn't say the words, but she thought about the question that plagued her mind. What would happen to the clan? Who would take his place? *What about you Abigale… what would become of you?* Too many unanswered questions lay heavy on her heart.

Marcus held her tight, "I'm sorry, I dinnae mean to upset ye. James is a warrior. I have seen him wounded before and he's too stubborn to die. He'll make it, Abigale."

Abigale looked up at him with tears streaming down her cheeks. Before she could apologize for breaking down, Marcus cupped her face, wiping away her tears.

Abigale began to feel uncomfortable as he gazed profoundly into her eyes as if he was in deep thought. He stayed there holding her a little too long and a little too close for her liking. Ill at ease, Abigale stepped out of his embrace.

Clearing his throat, Marcus asked, "When was the last time ye ate? I'll bring ye some of Alice's famous oatcakes."

"That would be very kind of ye."

Marcus turned on his heels and headed for the door.

Relieved he was leaving, Abigale had other things on her mind than to think about Marcus's odd behavior. Aye, he was a handsome man with a witty side, yet his honor was beginning to be questioned. Surely she'd seen something more than friendship in those blue eyes of his? Furthermore, he had overstayed his welcome. A man cannot take what has already been claimed.

Abigale shook herself from those thoughts. Perhaps she was misjudging him. After all, James was his cousin; maybe he needed to be consoled as well.

"Marcus," Abigale called out.

He turned to face her. "Lady Abigale."

"Thank ye."

Marcus smiled, nodded his head, and walked out the bedchamber.

Abigale walked over to James's bedside. She ran her fingers through his hair, bent down, and touched her forehead with his. "Come back to me," she whispered.

~~~~~

James blinked away the spinning room as it slowly came into focus. He heard soft breathing and lifted his head up slowly toward the noise. There she was; with one arm tucked under her head, Abigale slept. Trying to determine whether he was dreaming or not, he rubbed his thumb over her delicate hand that held onto his. Her hand felt soft and warm. This was a good sign, he thought.

Reaching out he took Abigale's braid in his hand. As he fondled the silky strands, a wave of relief rippled through him. Laying his head back down, he closed his eyes. He wasn't dreaming this time, His *bel ange* was here and safe.

The dream had been too real this time. He was ready to succumb to the darkness, yet something or better yet someone had stopped him. The light, aye the warm, bright light had chased away the collector. His soul was saved for now. Yet another question burned him. Why had Abigale been there in his dream?

James looked back down at Abigale again. He brushed her cheek with the back of his hand. "God's bones!" She was a beauty.

Sleepy eyes blinked open and became wide with excitement. "James, ye're awake."

"Aye." James coughed through the dryness in his throat.

Abigale slowly lifted her head. "Do ye remember what happened?"

Groaning in pain, James leaned forward. There was a tightness in his chest and he could feel the nausea roll through his gut. What the hell happened to him? His body felt battered, yet the pain was beginning to dull a bit.

"Easy." Abigale warned as she propped pillows behind James's back to make him more comfortable. "Ye were shot with an arrow two days ago while hunting. 'Twas an accident."

"Two days?"

"Aye."

"An accident… while I was hunting?" James's dark brows creased. This information didn't set well with him. He looked down at the blood-stained bandages. *Two days?* He should have healed by now. His sleep magic should have healed him quickly, not over two days. Never before had he come this close to death. The whole thing didn't make sense to him. He was endless… dateless… immortal. One blow from an arrow was like getting a splinter under your skin.

He'd remembered the burn of something flowing through his veins and even now he was in a tremendous amount of pain. *Poison?* Aye, he had to have been poisoned.

"If the arrow was an inch deeper… it would have reached yer heart."

James took Abigale's hand in his. "Ye're a healer?"

Abigale shrugged her shoulders, "Just a nurse with some knowledge in surgery."

"A surgeon?" This puzzled him. Usually women were discouraged and not allowed to practice surgery.

Abigale reached over to feel his head for fever and was stopped quickly. James grabbed her slender wrist as if he was done with her fussing over him. "How did you become a surgeon?"

Pulling her arm away from him, she said, "At the abbey, I spent a lot of time assisting the physicians and surgeons in the infirmary. Fortunately for ye, I'm one of the best surgeons the abbey had." She smiled.

James knew that she'd lived at Dunfermline Abbey, but for how long he did not know. Never really asking her about her time there, it dawned on him that he really didn't know Abigale at all and this saddened him.

For some strange reason he wanted to know everything about her. He could have died not knowing the woman who'd saved his life.

Abigale swallowed hard. "James, I... couldn't help but notice when I was removing the ---"

At that very moment Marcus stepped into the room interrupting their conversation with a plate of oatcakes and with Alice trailing close behind.

"My Laird, ye're awake! Oh tis a glorious day!" Alice beamed with delight and rushed over to James's bedside. "Lady Abigale brought ye back to us." Alice glanced at Abigale as they shared a smile.

At that moment the rest of his kinsmen came rushing into the bedchamber. Good news sure did spread fast. Rory's smile reached ear to ear as he looked at his chief. "Lucky bastard."

James returned his smile. "Aye."

He hated the fact that they were interrupted; he wasn't done with the questions he wanted to ask. Furthermore he needed to hold her... to feel her warmth. He studied her for a while. She looked exhausted. Had she been here with him the entire time?

As his men fussed over him, James kept his eyes on Abigale and watched her every move as Alice hugged her and gloated over the princess's healing abilities. His kinsmen, one by one, took their turn thanking her as well.

After the commotion settled he noticed Abigale walking toward the door to leave the bedchamber. "Abigale, where ye going?"

She turned back around. "I was going to look for a place to rest for a while. I'll be back soon."

"Nay lass, this is yer bedchamber. Ye'll sleep here." James had made his demands and motioned for everyone to take their leave.

"Are ye sure? I can find another room." Abigale worked her hands nervously into her apron.

Grinning a sexy smile, James pulled back the covers, offering her a warm place to snuggle. "My lady."

Deep blue eyes stared back at him. Abigale untied her bloodstained apron and slowly unlaced the front of her dress until she wore her shift. Intently watching her as she crawled on to the bed, James motioned for her to come closer. Dropping his view to her chest, he could see straight down her under dress to two perfectly round breasts that he begged to touch. By the saints, this lass was going to be the death of him. With smoldering eyes he traced her body back to her face. The dark skin under her eyes showed just how exhausted she was. Damn him for thinking with his cock; she needed sleep.

Abigale laid her soft body next to his. Her warmth pulled him in and held him captive. Wanting to feel more of her, he pulled her closer until their bodies molded together. This tantalizing feeling was the same he'd felt back in his dream. It was like he was basking in the sun, soaking up its rays without a care in the world. Is this what Conall meant? A woman's love bringing peace? Love… well maybe he shouldn't go that far, but this sensation he felt was like paradise.

He knew he was probably being selfish by wanting her next to him instead of letting her sleep by herself. Truth be told, when Abigale was around she chased his demons away. Firsthand he'd seen it, there was no doubt that she was the one who had chased the soul collector away. No nightmares… no soul collector to be found; she was the light to his darkness. James closed his eyes and kissed the top of Abigale's head. "Sweet dreams my *bel ange*."

Knowing where his demon hid, he would take these moments, cherish them, and put them to memory; only to recall them to remind him of who he was… a dragon. It wouldn't work out between them. How could it? She was human and he was Dragonkine. As soon as she found out the truth, she would be gone. No man with his amount of

110

uncontrollable vengeance could possibly be honorable enough to deserve a happy life. The English had taken so much from him that he feared that no matter how much blood was shed it would never be enough. Even if, and that was a big if, she could forgive his evil ways, there still lay a huge problem between them... he was a dragon. A young Dragonkine that needed the thrill of battle in order to quench his dragon's lust for blood and vengeance. Joining the king's rebellion allowed him to tame the beast.

Even with his bad reputation, his enemies were out there, he knew it... he welcomed it. This was why he vowed to never take a wife. Just the thought of something happening to Abigale in retaliation for his wrong-doings stirred a sinister feeling deep inside him that left him restless. Which led him to believe that this was no accident. Nay, the arrow being this close to his heart was no accident at all, he'd been a target. Unease settled in his bones; someone had tried to kill him, but who had taken the shot? Undoubtedly, the attacker had to have known he was Dragonkine, for he used a poison arrow. No mortal arrow could kill a dragon. Furthermore, the marksman was quite skillful with his bow, an accurate shot indeed.

James stiffened and held Abigale closer. Could there be a weed in the garden that needed to be pulled? A kinsman betraying not only their clan, but betraying the whole secrecy of the Dragonkine Guard? James ground his teeth together as he thought about one of his brethren turning on him. He needed to talk with Magnus soon.

Chapter 13

If you can't take the heat, don't tickle the dragon. ~ *Anonymous*

"Och lass." James tightened his muscles and sucked in a deep breath. "Touch me like that again and I'll have ye on your back quicker than I can draw my sword." He arched a brow. Even though he didn't want a wife he still very much desired the auburn-haired lass. The last two days had proven to him that he indeed liked Abigale's company and it didn't help that his dragon was relentless with his needs as well. He made himself known by stirring inside James's body, insisting to be around Abigale.

"Ye mean like this." Abigale blushed as she skimmed her fingers across his ribs teasing him as she unwrapped his bandages.

James squirmed in reaction to Abigale's tickling assault. "Aye, *bel ange.*" If only his men could see him now chuckling like a wee lad, they would jest him relentlessly. Truth be told he craved her touch a little more than he had the right to.

"My father speaks French, though I never learned. It's a beautiful language." She smiled. "He would call me his bel Abigale when he would come visit me at the nunnery. I cherished his visits especially not knowing when he would call again."

James noticed how Abigale's mood seemed to sadden when she talked about her father. He put his finger under her chin and lifted her head up so he could stare into her deep blue eyes. "Pas aussi belle que vous." James smiled. *Indeed, not as beautiful as ye,* James thought. "My father sent me, my younger brother, and mother to live in Paris when I was nine years old. He wanted our family safe and far away from the English." James huffed in annoyance. "Bloody Sassenach made my father surrender Castle Douglas and in return they let me, Archie and my mother leave unharmed."

"What happened to yer father?"

"My father was left to rot at the Tower of London. They called it a traitor's death." Hatred lingered on his every word.

"I'm so sorry, James," Abigale consoled him.

"Aye, me too." He changed the subject quickly, for bringing up that part of his past was no good. He already felt his dragon growling. "I can assure ye Abigale, if yer da could have he would have come to see ye more."

"Would have, could have, doesnae matter anymore. He had the chance to make it up to me and well—"

"He married ye off to the Bogeyman." James saw it in her eyes; she too did not want this marriage.

"I dinnae mean it that way. I'm happy here." She looked up from the bandage and smiled.

Abigale unwrapped the last bandage. "Hmmm." Her brows furrowed as she felt around the wound, examining it.

"What?"

"James, yer wound is healed," Abigale informed him.

He'd forgotten about his healing abilities. No wonder she looked shocked and confused. "Well, that's because I had an excellent nurse."

"But, the severity of yer wound—"

"Abigale, ye healed me." His tone was firm.

Knowing better than to push James, Abigale changed the subject. "What was Paris like?"

Bloody hell, what was with all the questions? This part of his life he'd as soon like to forget. Details of his life in Paris were difficult to explain and now wasn't the time to discuss it with her. He wouldn't know where to begin, for he'd gone through hell. His mother had died a few months after arriving. Some said it was the black plague that took her, but James knew differently. She'd died of a broken heart. Elizabeth loved his father so much that she couldn't live without him. Knowing that her husband was most likely dead or imprisoned, she had fallen into a deep depression and died.

After his mother's death, he and his brother were left to fend for themselves. Poor and with nowhere to go, they lived in the back alleys of Paris barely surviving. Up until that point, James had been strong and took care of wee Archie, always making sure Archie ate his fill first while James went without most nights. But fate had changed their roles, when James had become sick and his wee brother had to take care of him. James fought a burning fever, agonizing body aches, and violent vomiting. It had been two miserable weeks and he was weak and scared. For sure he'd thought the plague was taking his life.

It had been a cold, dreary winter in Paris, making it impossible to find a warm place to lay your head. With the spread of the black plague, no one took their chances bringing strangers in from the frigid weather. Surely if Archie hadn't made the decision to find shelter at a nearby church, they would have frozen to death.

James, as weak as he was, could barely walk through the thick snow covered ground. Falling into the thick powder, James could no longer bear his own weight. "Ye must go, Archie." His breath was visible through the flurries. "Leave me here. I will only slow ye down."

"Nay, Jamie." Archie bent down and propped his brother's arm around his neck. "Ye're all I have left. We go together."

James leaned on his younger brother, as they struggled through the unforgiving weather and made it to the steps of the church. Once inside they met a bishop who took the two frigid lads in and fed them a hot meal. As fate would have it, Bishop Andrews had been waiting for this day to come. It was written in the scrolls that it was his destiny to train and care for a dragon.

The massive clock tower at the church was secluded, a perfect place to house James as he went through his transformation to Dragonkine. As the dragon took over his body, bones popped, liquid lava burned through his veins, and raw uncontrolled power surged through him. James remembered how violently sick he was, and the pain was unbearable. This part of his life was off limits, sealed up tight, and never to be opened.

James felt a warm hand covering his arm and saw Abigale leaning toward him. "Ye dinnae have to tell me, James. I understand, the past is the past."

Indeed he did want to tell her everything in hopes she would accept who he was, but sheltering her from the truth was the logical thing to do.

"But," she interrupted the silence, "ye do have to tell me what *bel ange* means."

James moved closer to the edge of the bed so Abigale was standing between his legs. Two huge hands reached up, cupped her face, and pulled her closer. James stroked the tops of her cheeks softly with his thumbs and rested his forehead to hers. She had the most beautiful deep blue eyes. "It means beautiful angel."

Pressing his lips to Abigale's, he kissed her gently at first until her mouth opened, reassuring him that she indeed wanted his kisses. He plunged his tongue deeper inside her mouth, dominating the kiss and she matched his rhythm lick for lick. Heat flooded through him and his cock hardened as she ran her hands up and down his shoulders to his neck. His dragon roared, vibrating his core. Wanting to feel more of her, he pulled her closer until the softness of her breasts pressed up against his bare chest searing his flesh. James ran his hands down her back stopping at her tiny waist. If he didn't stop now he wouldn't be able to.

He grabbed her skirts, trying to contain the desire and douse the flames. He pulled away and stopped the kiss. He pressed his forehead to hers. "Abigale, ye make me want things I can no have."

Abigale whispered, "Whatever ye're going through please let me help. Please let me in."

James closed his eyes and wished it was that easy. He wanted to tell her everything and be rid of his burdens, but that wouldn't be fair to her. Lust wouldn't win over logic.

Still holding on to Abigale's waist, he looked up into her eyes. "I feel like I'm too close to the edge and about to--"

Abigale firmly grabbed his face between her hands. "Then jump. I'll catch ye."

James tightened his strong chiseled jaw and damned himself for a fool. Pulling her on top of him, he leaned back on the bed bringing her with him. He grabbed her arse tight and heard her moan. All control was lost and pure desire took over as he rolled her over on her back. He kissed her neck and pulled down her dress so he could feast his eyes on her beautiful breasts. He flicked his tongue over a pink nipple and sucked until it became hard. Abigale moaned in pleasure, encouraging James to keep up with his wicked assault on her body.

He'd never hungered for a woman like he hungered for Abigale. Feeling like the greedy bastard he was, he was going to take what she offered, make love to her until his name was screaming from her mouth. She was his wife, so bedding her was his rightful duty. Aye?

In a lust-crazed frenzy, James pulled up her skirts, all the while kissing her breasts. His hands finally reached her bare legs. Bare legs?

The lass wore no hose. He paused for a moment and cocked a brow at Abigale. "Yer hose?"

Abigale unleashed an innocent shy smile and shrugged. "I was hot."

That smile so pure, yet devious sent him further spiraling out of control. Reaching the waist of her undergarment, he slid his hand down over her womanhood and… by the saints, he burned for her.

~~~~~

Abigale completely lost herself in James's wicked ways; he'd awakened a deep desire she never knew she had. His kisses burned her flesh and his touch lit the fire that heated her core. She thought she would go up in flames when she felt his hand on her sex.

Disbelief set in as she thought about pinching herself to make sure she wasn't dreaming. Except she couldn't will her hands away from exploring the expanse of his broad shoulders, and the ridged peaks and valleys of his well-defined body. It was as if she was a prisoner under his control and she had no plans on escaping.

A voice off in the distance broke her thoughts as she heard a young boy call out to Fergus.

"Fergus?" she said out loud.

James halted his assault on her neck and looked down at her. "Och lass, that's not the name I wanted to hear from ye," he smirked. "I was thinking maybe James or better yet Laird Douglas of Angus take me now ye--"

"Shhh. I think I heard someone call out to Fergus." She lifted her head and cocked it to the side, straining to hear the voice again. God, was she going daft? A beautiful man was about to make love to her and she was hearing voices? Nay, she could have sworn she heard his name.

Discarding the distraction, Abigale pushed her hands through James's hair pulling him down into a mind blowing kiss as she forgot about everything and focused on the moment at hand.

A voice louder than the last rang through her passion-filled fog. This time she heard it crystal clear; she was not crazy. She pulled away from the kiss and tried to talk between panting breaths. "Did ye hear it?" She tried to raise herself up beneath James's weight, but it was pointless. James wasn't letting her go.

"Nay." James kissed down her neck and continued driving her crazy like the outside world didn't exist.

Abigale heard the voice again and this time she was sure she wasn't going daft. She heard Fergus's name. "James, please stop." At least that's what her mouth said but her body told him another story. "I need to see what's going on."

With a huff, James rolled over, letting Abigale escape. Readjusting her dress, Abigale slipped out of bed and walked to the window overlooking the bailey. Still trying to gather her thoughts, she fumbled with the fur covering the window. Once she found the opening, she peeked out and couldn't believe her eyes. "Oh no!"

James shot up into a sitting position on the bed. Well, he gave it his best effort, for his cock was hard as a rock and his body was aching for release. "What is it?" he growled.

"Fergus has run away from his stall and Niven is trying to catch him. I must go." Abigale began to search the chamber for her shoes. There was no time to waste, the lad was going to end up hurting himself; Fergus never allowed anyone but her to handle him.

Aha! She found her shoes. Balanced on one foot, she began to put on her slippers. "I'm sorry, James but if I dinnae go and calm Fergus down he will end up hurting Niven. I can no let that happen."

James let out a frustrated huff. "I assure ye Niven can handle Fergus. Now come back to bed, I'm no done with ye, lass."

Abigale shot her husband a ye-can-no-be-serious look as she slipped on her other shoe.

"Och, I suppose ye're right," James said in defeat.

"I'll be right back." Abigale smiled at James as he melted back down into the bed. *God's Blood the lass better hurry back!*

~~~~~

James lay there for a moment as he processed everything that was happening. By all that was holy that horse was spoiled rotten and was in desperate need of manners. He made a mental note about discussing this issue with Abigale. Fergus was going to have to behave in order to stay in the stable.

Shite. Realization smacked him upside the head; he'd forgotten, before leaving for the hunting trip two days ago, that he'd instructed the stable groom to prepare for Abigale's trip to her new home at Bothwell Castle. He'd planned to tell Abigale as soon as he got back, but what he didn't plan on was being shot with a poisonous arrow and his *bel ange* saving his life. Now that he wanted her to stay, he might have just blown the whole thing.

James shot out of bed panicked. "Abigale wait!" Quickly, he fetched his tunic and readjusted his trews. He had to stop her before she reached Niven and Fergus. Stubbing his toe on his way out of the bedchamber, James stumbled down the corridor, cursing along the way. God, he hoped he would catch her in time.

~~~~~

Abigale entered the bailey swiftly and ran over to Niven just in time as Fergus reared up on his hind legs and threatened to knock him down. "Are ye alright, lad?"

His voice shaking, Niven said, "Aye my lady, me sorry to have disturbed ye."

"'Tis alright," she reassured the frightened lad. "Fergus is just scared. Everything will be fine."

The fine steed settled as soon as Abigale approached. "Shh." She reached out her hand, patting his nose then moved to his muscular chest. The horse's chest pumped up and down and glistened with sweat. "Easy laddie, no one will hurt ye." Abigale calmed Fergus instantly. "What happened, Niven? Why is Fergus out of his stall?"

Niven looked down at his worn shoes and gripped his tunic tightly. "I'm only doing what the Laird Douglas has instructed."

"And just what has the laird instructed ye to do?"

The lad paused and swallowed hard.

"'Tis ok. Ye may speak freely," Abigale reassured him. "No harm will come to ye."

"My lady, I'm to ready yer horse for the trip to Bothwell."

"Bothwell?" Did she hear the lad right? Why would James want to send Fergus to Bothwell? This just didn't make any sense.

"Aye," the shaken voice answered.

"And why would he be going to Bothwell when his home is here with me?" Abigale's tone was gracious, yet firm.

"My lady, I'm to ready yer horse and escort ye to Bothwell. We leave in the morn."

Shocked didn't come close to describing her reaction. James was sending her away? To Bothwell? Not wanting to frighten Niven more than he already was she bent down and took the lad's trembling hands in hers. "I assure ye, I will be staying here. This is my home. Fergus should be fine now. Take him back to his stall now and leave him be. I promise I'll have a talk with him about his attitude." She smiled.

Niven nodded his head and quickly began his task.

Abigale stood up with her hands on her hips, and turned to find her husband barreling through the bailey towards her. He must have known he was too late, for he treaded softly as he approached. She could feel her cheeks had reddened with anger… no, fury was more like it. "Bothwell, as in Bothwell Castle?"

Abigale, Let me explain," James begged.

Abigale stood there for a while deciding whether or not she wanted to hear his excuses. Nay… nay, in fact she didn't want to hear what he had to say. It had dawned on her that no matter what he said to her right now, she no longer cared. Hurt, pure and painful, stabbed at her heart. He was going to send her away; how could he do this to her?

No longer containing her anger she pushed herself past him and started toward Black Stone; with each step her anger grew.

Desperately trying to stop her, James followed a step behind trying to get her attention, but she kept tracking forward with purpose. "Abigale, please stop and listen to me."

Ignoring his words, she reach the great hall doors. They entered the hall like a wind storm blowing in. "Damn it, would ye stop for one second and listen to me!" James grabbed her arm and swung her around until she looked at him.

Blinding rage took over every fiber of her being. If he thought for a minute she was going to listen to him he was seriously mistaken. She ripped her arm from his grip and allowed every raw emotion she'd felt since the day she met the Black Douglas to wash over her in rolling raging waves. One by one she released them until she felt the world lift from her shoulders. "Nay James Douglas, heed my words and hear them well. I've been more than agreeable in accepting my fate being married to ye. I've given up my morals and lied to a priest. I practically threw myself at ye thinking maybe... just maybe ye would desire me." She swallowed past the lump in her throat and fought back the tears. "I've given ye all that I have, to only be shut out by yer stubborn as a mule ways." She paused and took a deep breath. Gaining more courage she squared her shoulders and continued. "I'm tired of being shut out. If ye think ye're going to send me away to Bothwell so ye do no have to deal with whatever is going on in that head of yers, ye had better think again."

"Abigale, just let me –"

She looked up at the towering beast and pinned him hard with an ice cold stare. "If ye do no want to be around me then ye leave. I'm staying here." With that said Abigale turned on her heels, strode across the great hall, and climbed up the stairs straight to her bedchamber.

~~~~~

James stood dumbfounded. Every word spoken was true. Abigale showed him more love then he deserved. Though she'd been wrong about one thing; he did desire her. From the moment he met her at the loch he knew he loved her. Problem was she sent him spinning out of control, and he had been desperate to escape whatever bewitching spell she cast upon him.

There was no way around the matter; he had to make her listen to him. If he had to lock her in their bedchamber and hold her down, the lass would hear him out. He cursed himself and began to take off after Abigale when a soft but sturdy grip held his arm. "Nay, let her go," Alice said.

James closed his eyes. "Alice, let me go. I have to talk to her."

"I can no let ye do it. If ye go after her now ye'll make a bigger arse out of yerself then ye have already." Alice motioned for James to sit at a nearby table. "If there's one thing I know, it's when a lass needs her space ye give it to her."

James took a seat and rested his head in his hands, scrubbing the tension from his temples. "Alice, I've been a fool."

"Aye, a fool in love." Alice patted him on his shoulder and placed a plate of special oatcakes in front of him followed by a tankard of mead.

Oh how he'd missed Alice. She always knew what to say at the right time, soothing him just like a mother would do. But, step out of line and she'd let you have it. He grabbed an oatcake and took a bite out of it. "Mmm, 'tis good."

Alice sat down beside him and rested her hands on the table in front of her. Her face grew serious. "James, ye be a good man. Dinnae let yer past spoil yer future with Lady Abigale."

"'Tis not the past I worry about so much as my better half." He turned to Alice and flashed his dragon's eyes. "She'll never understand."

"Aye, but did ye give her a chance to try to understand it? She's a smart woman, James and she's good for ye too." She winked.

Aye, she was perfect in every way. Even when she was mad she was graceful. "I need to talk to her." James began to stand up and leave when Alice clucked her tongue at him. "'Tis best ye wait until the morn, trust me words. She's hurt, she thinks ye're abandoning her."

James sat back down. "Abandoning her?"

"Aye. 'Tis not my story to tell but Abigale's da didnae visit her much at the abbey. She told me she felt abandoned by her da. So, ye can see why she feels like ye're doing the same."

James was stunned. Instead of thinking how this would affect her, he had been too wrapped up in his own reasonings for sending her away. The look on Abigale's face when he mentioned her da came filtering through his mind. She wanted to shut this part of her life out just like he wanted to shut out his dragon side from her.

"Alice, I've been a selfish stubborn arse."

Alice shook her head, "Ye be a Dragonkine and there's no fault in that." Alice stood from the table, "Now go to yer solar and think wisely about yer situation. Talk to Abigale in the morn after a good night's rest. Trust me." She smiled and quit the hall.

James grabbed another oatcake and headed to the solar. *Think wisely*, he mused. Words never seemed to come easy for him when it came to expressing himself, especially when it came to Abigale. But he had to try to make her see that indeed he wanted her to stay and that he would never abandon her, ever. Even if she denied his dragon, he would always love and protect her.

Chapter 14

Ye be no princess, ye're a bastart!

Abigale slammed the wooden door to the bedchamber with such force she thought she heard the hinges crack. "Unbelievable," she muttered out loud as she paced the room. Here she was on the verge of being abandoned again; sent away, unwanted, and left to live alone. Her mother had left her when she died… abandoned, her father had left her at the nunnery… abandoned, and now her husband wanted to send her away to Bothwell. *Nay, I won't leave.*

Something had changed between them in the past few days, she felt it. James wouldn't let her out of his sight, so they had spent most of the day cuddled in bed while James healed and Abigale caught up on sleep. He'd fed her with the prepared provisions that Alice had brought up to them. Recalling the way he would rub his hands up and down her back comforting her while she slept, she knew he cared for her. His kisses felt like she was the only woman he had ever kissed, slow but with fierce need. There was something more between them and there was no denying it. Well, at least on her part there was no denying.

Or had she played the fool? Abigale's anger grew. Was this some kind of trickery or bewitchment? Had she been too blind to see that he was a man who took what he wanted and didn't care about anyone else? Could he be so cruel as to have his pleasures with her then send her off and be done with her? Mayhap he would only call on her to satisfy his urges. His own personal whore. Even though they were married, the thought alone made her feel like a whore.

Why was fate being so cruel to her? Didn't she deserve happiness? Or mayhap she didn't, perhaps her destiny was to be alone. *Alone and a bastard.* Abigale stopped in mid-stride as a vision of Abbess Margaret appeared over by the hearth. The raven-haired Abbess turned slowly to face Abigale. Her voice chilled her like ice. "Did ye actually think that a man would want ye, bastart?" Abbess Margaret seethed.

Abigale back-stepped until her back hit the door. "Nay, ye cannae be here." Every word she spoke shook with fear.

In a split second the Abbess was eye to eye with Abigale. "Oh I'm real, I'll never leave. Ye need me to remind ye of who ye truly are. A bastart that's all alone," she mocked. "If ye were a true princess yer father wouldn't have abandoned ye."

"Nay." Abigale shook her head back and forth as she slid down the door. Huddled into a quivering ball, she hugged her legs close to her body waiting for her hair to be coiled around the Abbess's deadly fist.

The wretched woman towered over Abigale's shaking body. "The only reason James married ye was because it was arranged by ye father. Yer father didnae want ye so he married ye off to be done with ye. Ye be no princess, ye're a bastart!"

Abigale fisted her hands and began to hit herself in the head to make the voice stop. "Please, stop!" *Dear God, please make it stop.* This wasn't happening, not now. Normally she was able to fight back and make the vile woman stop. She thought that once she had left the abbey she would no longer be plagued by the evil woman. But as fate would have it, she was a bastard and abandoned again.

Abigale banged her fists harder against her temples. "I'm no bastart," she cried out and repeated to herself over and over again until she could no longer hear the Abbess's words. When silence filled the room, Abigale dared to open her eyes. As she opened one eye at a time, relief washed over her as an empty bedchamber came into view. Quickly Abigale jumped to her feet and ran to the window, pushing the furs out of the way. She was sure she would see the Abbess fly from her window and back to her lair like some kind of night creature.

The walls of Castle Black Stone were beginning to feel constricting and her chest felt tight. She needed to leave this place for a while and clear her head. Mayhap a trip into the village would do her some good. Never being able to leave on her own will, excitement grew as she thought about what she might see. Perhaps some sweet smelling candles would lighten her mood. Abigale grabbed her cloak and headed for the door.

Once in the corridor, she lost herself in her current state of anger, she wasn't aware of her surroundings and didn't notice Marcus walking behind matching her stride. "See, I told ye he was too stubborn," Marcus mused.

Startled that she was being followed, Abigale stopped abruptly to turn and face Marcus. "What is it with ye Highlanders sneaking up on people?" Beyond irritated at this point, her tongue was quick to insult.

Taken aback by the firmness of her tone, Marcus stepped back. "Lady Abigale, please forgive my rudeness. I was just trying to lighten yer mood."

Truly he seemed sincere. Abigale felt horrible for snapping at him. It wasn't his fault that his cousin was an arse. "Marcus, I'm afraid I'm in no mood for company right now. Please excuse me, the mood in here is foul and I need some fresh air."

They continued onward. Reaching the stairs, Abigale descended steadfastly to the great hall. True to being who he was, a Highlander, Marcus wasn't taking no for an answer. He followed her a few steps behind. "Ye know I'm a good listener and ye look as if ye need to speak yer mind about something."

Nay, she didn't need an ear, she needed to be away from this castle and most definitely away from a stubborn man. She'd had enough of being told what to do and when she was going to do it. She was hurt, confused, and mourned the fact she might possibly be leaving Alice and Effie.

Abigale took a deep breath trying to rein in her fury. "I thank ye kindly for yer concern, but I need to be alone right now. I'm taking Fergus to the village. I need some time to clear my head." She tried her best to smile and reassure him that she would be fine, she needed some time... alone.

"The village... alone... without an escort! Nay, won't allow it." Marcus folded his arms in front of his chest as if saying ye'll leave over my dead body.

"Och... I... I won't be gone long. I'll be fine."

"Nay lass, ye cannae go alone, 'tis not safe. The merchants can be ruthless out there. And do I need to mention the natty lads lurking around waiting to pick your pockets. I'll escort ye to the village."

It was true, merchants could be ruthless; desperate people did desperate things. With last winter being relentlessly frigid then adding to spring's saturating rains, the terrain conditions for farming in the Highlands had become a challenge. Livestock froze to death and the soil was unproductive. Most items they had were brought back from village raids or crusades. People were hungry and in need of coin.

His mouth was just inches from her ear. He whispered, "I will nay take no for an answer."

The sound of his deep baritone voice made Abigale go silent. His presence alone demanded submission like he was never denied it. Unease shivered through her, as she felt his hot breath searing her neck.

"Good. I'll tell the stable groom to ready the horses for us. We'll leave shortly." Marcus strode out of the great hall taking all the tension with him, leaving Abigale to settle her nerves.

Feeling even more irritated, Abigale blew out a pent up breath. All she wanted right now was to be alone with her thoughts. Making her way to the kitchen, she remembered that she'd hid her dirk under one of the large black cauldrons. Not needing its use, she had hid it there before she went to bathe Lennox and Mahboon. Thank God the cauldron had been cold and unused this morn. Bending down, she looked under the pot. Reaching with all her might, her hand touched cold steel. *Aye, my dirk.*

Lifting the right side of her dress thigh high, she attached a black strap around her leg and sheathed the blade. Relieved her dirk was securely strapped to her inner thigh, she patted down her skirts and made her way to the stables, but before she left she grabbed an apple for Fergus.

As they reached the village, the aftermath of the hard rainfalls was hard to miss. The small village had been beaten and bruised; dirt paths had been washed away leaving behind dried ripples of mud. Water collected in small pools that dotted the paths weaving through the town. Rocks and stones had been unearthed by the flooding rain making it hard to walk without tripping and the stench of wet thatch was everywhere.

Abigale couldn't believe how much destruction the rains had left behind. On the other hand, the clan members' attitude didn't match their muddled living conditions. The town came alive as villagers were patching up missing thatch from their roofs, cattle were being moved to drier ground, and merchants were out with carts full of salvaged vegetables and furs for the winter to come.

Abigale and Marcus walked through the merchant area of the village observing the different items for sale or barter. Her attitude began to soften a bit. Fresh air really did help clear the mind. Plus, Marcus hadn't pushed the issue for her to talk about what ailed her. Indeed he'd held true to his word and kept quiet, but was ready to listen when Abigale was ready to talk.

Out of the corner of her eye, Abigale spotted a heavy-set older woman stepping out from behind a cart selling what looked like fresh honey. The woman approached Abigale, but was quickly halted by Marcus's sword before she reached. The woman swallowed hard.

"Pardon me my lady, I only want to thank ye for saving Laird Douglas." She bowed her head and nervously wadded up her apron in her hands.

Abigale motioned for Marcus to release the woman, she held no threat. The woman lifted her head to look at Abigale. "My lady, I do no have expensive gifts to give, but would ye kindly accept this as a token of my gratitude?" The woman handed Abigale a cloth covered object that fit in the palm of her hand.

Abigale was shocked when she opened the fabric and found a brooch. Abigale ran her finger around the half circle pendant tracing the knot work. The brooch was weathered and looked old as though it had been passed down through generations.

"Oh my lady, watch oot for the pointy end. 'Tis sharp," the woman warned.

Amazed that the woman would part with such an heirloom, Abigale could not accept such a gift. "I can no—"

Marcus interrupted Abigale before she made a huge mistake. Refusing a gift was an insult. "The princess thanks ye kindly."

Abigale stood dumbfounded. She felt guilty for accepting such an elaborate gift.

As they walked away, Abigale felt confused as she looked over her shoulder at the woman who was now beaming with a smile. Why would she give her such a gracious gift when a simple thank you would suffice?

Marcus leaned his head toward Abigale as they walked side by side. "'Tis rude to decline a gift, especially when it's a gift of thanks."

Bewildered, she turned back around. "Marcus, she could have used this trinket to barter for food or at least a few coos."

"Aye, but she wanted ye to have it." Marcus winked at her.

It was apparent that Abigale had a lot to learn about life. Being sheltered came with its disadvantages, she thought. Clan rules hadn't existed in her world until a few days ago. She would have felt horrible if she'd hurt the poor woman's feelings by not accepting her gift. Being naïve was going to land her in a world of trouble if she didn't watch it.

As they passed the last merchant Abigale noticed a rundown stone dwelling with a badly woven thatch roof. Two little girls with ripped, dirty tunics were standing outside in front of a loosely hung door that banged shut with every light breeze that blew through the village. The little girls were filthy and looked as if they hadn't eaten or slept for days.

Before Marcus could stop Abigale, she walked up to the girls and bent down to their level. "Where's yer mum and da?"

The youngest girl swayed back and forth with her hands tucked behind her back. She looked down to her bare dirt-stained toes and shrugged her tiny shoulders. She had to be about five summers old, Abigale thought as she picked a piece of caked-on mud from the little girl's body. The eldest girl shoved her shoulder into the little girl as if letting her know not to trust the strangers.

Abigale walked past the girls and into their home, if you could call it a home. Cautiously, she pushed the door open and quickly had to cover her nose from the wretched smell that permeated the home. "Hello! Is anyone home? "Abigale yelled out. No one answered.

Marcus followed Abigale inside and quickly covered his nose with a white linen cloth. "Bloody hell!" He stood next to Abigale as they observed the filth. Rotten food and dirty trenchers littered a wooden table near the hearth which was blackened with thick soot. Straw mixed with mice droppings covered the dirt floor and in the middle of the small house lay a mud puddle. Abigale cringed at the thought that this was the only source of water for the girls. "Who would allow such living conditions?" She shook her head.

"I dunno. Something is verra wrong here." Marcus motioned for them to leave, for the stench was overpowering.

Abigale stepped back outside, breathing in the much-needed fresh air. The girls still stood where they were, watching them intently, yet never saying a word. Abigale's heart broke for these girls. Undoubtedly they had been mistreated and left alone to fend for themselves. But for how long? How could someone do such a thing? Something wasn't right here, Abigale could feel it.

"Marcus, we need to take these girls back to Black Stone. They can no stay here."

Marcus stood with his arms folded in front of him glaring at the girls as if he didn't trust this situation. "My lady, I think it's best we leave before someone shows up." He advised.

Abigale was shocked that he wanted to leave these poor defenseless girls here. Her dark brows furrowed in disbelief. "Ye dinnae mean to leave the girls here? We have to welcome them into our home until we figure oot what happened."

"Ye don't understand. If we take the girls, their parents may come looking for them. It could start a feud. Ye don't want to be charged with kidnapping… do ye?" Marcus was trying to talk some sense into her, but knowing Abigale's kind heart, he was losing the battle.

"I will no leave these girls." Abigale put her hands on her slender hips, tipped her chin up, and stood her ground. "Either I stay here," God, she hoped it didn't come to that, "or I bring the girls back to Black Stone. As long as I'm married to the laird, we'll take care of our people."

Marcus ran his hand through his rugged light brown hair in aggravation. "Fine, but ye will have to answer to yer husband, no me."

Abigale smiled in victory, but it was short-lived as the ground started to rumble and screams rang out. Full-on panic raced to life throughout

132

the village as its people started to scatter and run for their lives. Abigale turned to Marcus. His hand already palmed the hilt of his sword ready to protect her. As if he knew what she was going to ask, he informed her of what was going on. "Village raid. We need to get ye out of here, now!" Marcus bellowed through the screams and pounding hooves.

An orange glow lit up the sky. Flames raged as ruthless knights upon charging warhorses torched homes and crops to the ground. Abigale couldn't move. Everything was happening so fast as if she was dreaming. Marcus stood in front of her with his hands on her shoulders and gave her a shake to get her attention. "Lady Abigale, ye must leave. There's no time to waste." Something instinctual awakened and with much haste she picked the youngest girl up in her arms, while Marcus carried the eldest. Abigale followed him to a thick wooded area. Once they were deep inside the forest and away from the attack, Marcus put the girl down. She quickly ran to Abigale and found comfort in her skirts. "There's no time to get back to the castle. Ye'll have to hide in here until I come back for ye." Marcus gave the order true and firm.

"Where are ye going?" Surely he wasn't going to leave them here alone. Abigale couldn't fight off an attacker. Was he daft?

"I'm going back to the village. I need to alert James. Find a place to hide. I'll be back." Marcus headed back to the village.

Oh dear Lord, what was she going to do? Her heart was racing so fast she could hear its beats pounding in her ears. What to do... What to do? Abigale turned around, looking in every direction, trying to find a place to hide. Everything was happening so fast, her head started to spin.

Get it together Abigale Bruce, these girls are depending on ye. They need yer strength, not weakness, she scolded herself. Taking a deep breath she decided to head deeper into the forest. They came across an old yew tree with its trunk hollowed out. A perfect place to hide. Still carrying the wee girl in her arms, Abigale was beginning to feel fatigued. Finally they reached the huge tree trunk just before she thought her arms would give out beneath the heavy weight she carried. "We'll be safe here," she reassured the girls. The two girls clung tightly to one another as they sat toward the back of the hollowed yew. With haste Abigale removed her dirk and sat with the children. "Marcus will come back. I promise." She told herself this several times until she believed it. She put her arms around the girls, squeezing them tight. She kissed their heads, making sure they knew she wasn't going to leave them.

~~~~~

A massacre symphony played on with gut-wrenching cries of men and women being burned and slaughtered as the English garrison continued their raid with fierce determination on clan Douglas. Marcus dodged a man's claymore, then stuck the filth in the gut with the pointy end of his blade, as he made his way toward his horse. Abruptly a knight perched high upon his warhorse stopped Marcus with his sword pointed at Marcus's throat. Marcus swallowed against the cold steel and felt its prick. Long black feathers protruded from the top of the knight's helm and flowed down past his shoulders, whipped in the wind. Through the slit of his visor, his cold stare chilled Marcus bone deep. "Where's the princess, Highlander?" The knight shoved the blade deeper into Marcus's throat, just enough to prove his point.

Marcus studied the man for a while as if he was considering how he was going to answer. Or mayhap he was questioning his own motives.

The warhorse, foaming at the mouth and chomping at the bit, pawed the earth in irritation. "Well, are ye going to tell me or will I have to gut ye?" The knight seethed.

Marcus looked toward the woods where he'd left Abigale and the girls, then back at the impatient knight.

The Douglas war cry broke their stance as both men readied for battle. A cruel twisted smile reached across the knight's lips as he turned and faced the Black Douglas and two hundred of his clansmen.

~~~~~

Abigale was trying desperately to be brave, but if the truth be told she was just as scared as the girls. Time seemed to stand still. In the distance she could hear the blood-curdling cries of villagers, and the tiniest forest sounds seemed louder than they really were. Abigale grew restless. They couldn't stay hidden in here forever. What if something happened to Marcus? What if those raiders came searching for them? Nay, she couldn't stay here. She needed to find out what was going on.

"Girls, I'm going to take a look outside. I need for ye to be brave and stay here until I return," Abigale insisted. Both girls, with dirt-stained tears streaming from their faces, clung to one another, and the youngest shook her head no. Abigale wiped away the wee girl's tears. "I promise I won't be long, little lamb."

Before Abigale got up to leave, she looked down at her dirk. She couldn't leave the girls unprotected, she thought. Pushing her skirts up, she unsheathed her dirk and handed it to the eldest girl. "Here take this and dinnae be afraid to use it." She quit the yew tree hideaway.

Abigale reached the tree line, peeking through a thicket of blackthorn overlooking the village, and cringed. The sound of swords clanking together echoed through the screams as blood was being shed. Even though clan Douglas was fighting for their lives, there had been too many lives lost. Her heart told her she needed to help the wounded and tend to their wounds, but common sense told her to stay hidden and get back to the girls.

As she looked toward the castle gauging how far away it was, she noticed about two hundred clansmen on horseback riding toward the village. Thank God help was on the way! But where was Marcus? Dear God, please let him be alive.

She was retreating into the forest to her secret hideaway, when suddenly a strong rough hand grabbed her braid and yanked her into a hard ridged chest. "Aren't ye a pretty one?" A snarl came from the man as he snaked his arm around Abigale's waist and covered her mouth with his free hand. The repulsive man smelled like a dung heap and ale lingered on his breath. A raider indeed, Abigale thought. She planted her feet and tried to wriggle free. Not wanting to frighten the girls, Abigale held back her screams as panic pricked up her spine. What was this man going to do to her, better yet what was she going to do? She should have never left the safety of the yew tree.

As if by some kind of survival instinctual reaction, Abigale hauled-off and kicked at the man's shins and bit down hard on his hand until she tasted the tang of blood. If the man was going to have his way with her, she'd fight him until the end. "Ye bitch!" the raider yelled out in pain and released her. As he held his hand, shock spread across his scarred, unshaven face. The wench had the ballocks to fight him. An evil grin crept across his lips like he was ready and willing for the chase. "Ye better run little lamb before I catch ye," he sneered with hatred.

Not wanting to lead the foul man straight to the girls, Abigale turned and ran in the opposite direction from the yew tree. She pumped her legs through the unforgiving material of her dress that only seemed to slow her down. She glanced over her shoulder to find that the rogue was hot on her heels. An inconvenient stump and a misstep sent Abigale tumbling to the ground. Not a good predicament to be in. Quickly she turned over and frantically scooted backwards away from the raider. This was it, she thought.

"Looks like the big bad wolf caught ye wench. Ye'll pay for wounding me fighting hand." The man grabbed Abigale's legs and slid her towards him as he yanked up her dress.

Abigale strained to shove the man off her, but he was too strong. She pounded her fist into his chest and clawed at his face, but the raider fed off her distress. She kicked and twisted and through tear-filled eyes she saw a raised meaty hand coming towards her face to strike. Pulling up her arms to block the blow, she closed her eyes tight and braced herself. The man's hand came down and smacked her face causing stars to burst behind her eyes. Then another blow followed.

Coming to her senses wasn't easy as Abigale felt the wretched raider straddle her and untie his dirt-stained trews. "Ah, what a fine piece of arse we have here." He pushed his hips forward shoving his hardness against her stomach.

This couldn't be happening to her, this had to be a terrible nightmare. Her head throbbed and her body ached. *Abigale for God's sake, wake up!* A sharp prick poked at her chest as if she had been stung. The brooch that the woman from the village had given her. She had pinned it to her gown before she found the girls.

Oh my lady, watch oot for the pointy end. 'Tis sharp. The woman's voice echoed through her head. *Indeed, 'tis sharp*, Abigale mused. Quickly she reached for it and slipped it off her dress. With the pendant in the palm of her hand and the pointy end sticking straight up, she waited to make her move.

"Ye know wench, if ye just spread yer legs like a good little girl this would be over soon." The sickening mocking laughter he belted out made the bile rise up in her throat. *Come on ye eejit, make yer move.*

The foulness of his breath assaulted her senses as the raider bent down to roughly grab her breasts. Abigale pulled her arm back giving her just enough room to carry out the momentum she needed. She released her swing and plunged the sharp end of the brooch into the man's neck.

Wide-eyed, the man looked at her in shock. His hand covering the wound was dripping with blood. He made an attempt to yell at her but blood poured from his mouth. Time seemed to have stilled as she watched the raider holding his neck, trying to breathe.

In no time at all the man was yanked from Abigale's body by a massive man she recognized. *James?*

James stood behind the raider and grabbed him by his neck, snatching him off Abigale. He twisted the man around so that his body blocked Abigale's view of the raider and what he was about to do to him.

With one fluid motion and a loud crack, James snapped the raider's neck, letting his lifeless body fall to the ground.

James's eyes darkened and his face turned sinister as he looked down at Abigale. So, this was what the Black Douglas looked like. If she could disappear into the forest floor right now she would. This man was undoubtedly livid with her, but nonetheless she was happy to see him.

James extended a hand to Abigale and helped her up off the wet forest floor. "He hit ye?" James cradled her face in his hands and wiped the blood from the corner of her mouth.

Abigale was silent. She couldn't believe that she just stabbed a man. Seeing the man lying in a lifeless heap, she said, "Is he dead?"

"Dinnae look, Abigale. Look at me."

As soon as she looked up into his amber eyes, she began to crumble. She wrapped her arms around him and melted into his tight embrace as if he was the security she needed to help her forget about the blasted man and what he was going to do to her.

"Did he—"

Knowing what James was hinting at, Abigale shook her head. "Nay, I stabbed him with the brooch before he had the chance to."

They stood there for a while, holding on to one another. Abigale felt James's chest exhale in relief, yet he wasn't completely satisfied with the situation. By the way he flexed and worked his jaw, she knew James was angry. Once he knew she was alright no words had been spoken between them. Abigale stepped out from his embrace and began to brush the dirt from her dress.

"Are ye alright, lass?" James's tone was deep. He was concerned, yet she could sense the tenseness he held toward her.

Still angry at him over his last shenanigans, Abigale brushed him off. "Nay, I'm just a little rattled." She avoided eye contact, for she really didn't have the strength to fight with him. She needed to get back to the girls. "The girls." Abigale ran towards the yew tree praying that the girls were untouched.

James ran after her. "Wait… What girls are ye talking about?"

Chapter 15

Never mess with a dragon's woman.

The ride back to Black Stone was eerily quiet. James rode ahead of his men holding in his rage. He worked his jaw until he felt his teeth grind together, never once sparing a glance at Abigale, because he didn't trust himself not to come down hard on the lass. He was holding on by a fraying thread. Plus he didn't want to lose control in front of his men nor frighten the little girls who rode with Abigale.

If the lass would have just let him explain himself, she wouldn't have found herself in the middle of a village raid and… James stopped mid-thought and shook his head. He couldn't think about what that English filth was going to do to her. *God's wounds,* he had ripped the man's head clear off his shoulders with such viciousness. More like sliced it off. With claws extended, he cut the bastard just like a blade.

Then there was the issue of these wee girls coming to stay at Black Stone. There was no problem in taking care of your own, but with that came a risk. Who knew where or who their parents were?

As they approached the stables, James's anger started to boil over as he saw Marcus help Abigale and the girls dismount from Fergus. James rushed to the great hall. He needed mead.

Shortly after James had entered the hall, Abigale and the girls followed behind him with Rory, Conall, Magnus and Marcus.

"What were ye thinking, lass!" The baritone of his voice rang out in rage and echoed throughout the great hall.

Abigale quickly gave Alice the little girl in her arms. "Ye'll be safe with Alice," she reassured the girls. Alice lifted the wee child up and on to her hip. "Come along my sweets." Alice placed a comforting hand on the oldest girl's shoulder and led her to the stairs leading to a bedchamber. Abigale was sure that Alice was going to pamper the girls with a warm bath and food.

Marcus, Rory, Conall and Magnus came into the great hall to join them and silently waited for their laird's wrath. By the looks of it, it was going to be one hell of a battle of the strong-willed.

"Abigale!" The echo of her name being yelled made her shudder and sent a chill down her spine. James was furious with her.

Abigale closed her eyes and took a deep breath to settle her nerves before she faced the storm. As she turned around, she met an ice cold dark stare "My Laird," she swallowed, "I went to the village for some fresh air. As ye may recall, I needed some time to think about my new-found knowledge of Bothwell Castle."

James stood towering over her tiny frame, sternly looking down at her, his voice deep, low, and intimidating. "Ye wouldn't have needed fresh air if ye would've let me explain." James's jaw ticked in aggravation.

Abigale back-stepped until she felt the coldness of the stone wall on her back. James stalked toward her. "I didnae go alone… Marcus was with me," Abigale meekly replied.

James turned his head toward Marcus and if looks could kill, Marcus would be a corpse. "And ye thought this was a good idea? Going to the village when there could very well be someone out there wanting me dead?" Just that thought alone raised his fury to the next level.

Before Marcus could answer, Abigale interrupted. "James, it's no his fault, he tried to talk me out of it."

James braced his large hands on either side of Abigale's head, encaging her to the wall. Now she was defending Marcus. Like it wasn't bad enough she left Black Stone with another man, now she defended him. James looked as if he wanted to rip Marcus's heart out and feed it to his dogs. His dragon agreed and begged to be released.

One thing James was learning fast was you don't mess with a dragon's woman.

"I want ye to heed my words carefully, Abigale." James leaned his head down until their foreheads were slightly touching. His cold dark stare flickered with rage. "Ye will no leave Black Stone again. Is that clear?" James growled his demands deep and low.

She ducked down and freed herself from his entrapment. "I will no be a prisoner here. I shall come and go as I please."

The silence was deafening in the great hall, not even a breath was taken. Everyone waited for James's reaction. No one dared to defy a command from the laird.

Who did this lass think she was, denying his command? At first James didn't know how to respond. If one of his men were defiant he showed no mercy... off with their heads. But he couldn't very well do that to Abigale, though the thought of bending her over his knee and spanking her arse did.

"Ye do as I say."

Hands on her hips. "And what if I don't?" Abigale's cheeks flushed red with anger.

James approached Abigale dominating and demanding. He grabbed her arms to make a point that he wasn't taking no for an answer. "If I have to, I'll lock ye in the bedchamber... tie ye to the bed... I'll do whatever necessary to ensure yer safety. Do ye understand me?"

"James, leave the lass alone. If ye want to place blame then place it on me." Marcus began to walk toward James until he was standing face to face with him. Both men were the same height, but Marcus was leaner. His bright blue stare challenged James.

James didn't back down, he stood firm. "She is no business of yers, cousin. I suggest ye back down before someone gets hurt."

"Are ye threatening me?"

James's jaw ticked. The feelings running through him right now were foreign to him and he didn't know how to control them. However, it didn't help that his dragon was restless and itched for a fight. Jealousy wasn't an emotion he was used to.

"Nay, no threat. I'm just curious why the sudden interest in my wife. Do ye want her for yourself?"

Marcus smirked. "I can no deny the fact that she deserves a better man than ye."

Before Marcus knew what hit him, James shoved him with such power that Marcus stumbled back. Marcus threw his arms up as if he was beckoning James to take the first punch. He was not a coward and he didn't fear his cousin, not by a long shot. "Go ahead… make yer move, Laird Douglas," Marcus mocked.

James had had enough. Emotions of jealousy, anger, and confusion were running amok in his head. He didn't quite understand why Marcus was challenging him like this. Was he really trying to make an impression on Abigale? Or did he have other ulterior motives? Regardless, he was being challenged and knew he needed to decide what he was going to do about it. Oh, he knew damn well what his dragon wanted to do. Shred the bastard. Nay, he would grab ahold of whatever was left of his self-control and be a man and walk away. In time he would fix things between him and Abigale, because there was no way in bloody hell he would let her go.

James looked Marcus up and down as if he was disgusted by his mere being. He stayed silent and turned to walk away.

"Or are ye a coward like yer da?" Marcus pushed on.

James charged him, spearing his stomach with his right shoulder until his body slammed against the stone wall. Marcus's head bounced off the stone with a thud and he smirked at James with the devil in his eyes. He was mocking him again. Against James's will, he cocked his right arm back and his massive hand pummeled down on Marcus's face. He was going to make damn sure to knock that smirk off his face. James readied himself to repeat the assault on Marcus when he heard Abigale shriek, "Stop it!"

Abigale rushed over to James and held on to his arm before he could hit Marcus again. James pushed her off his arm and Abigale stumbled from the force. She tried again and stepped in front of James as Rory and Conall grabbed Marcus and escorted him outside. With all her might Abigale forcefully pushed her hands into James's rock solid chest. "This is quite enough!"

James snapped his attention to Abigale and looked down at her. His chest heaved up and down as his breathing labored and his hands were bloodied. His irises swirled amber with reptilian slits as pupils. A sinister stare pinned Abigale. He had lost all control and let his dragon take over.

~~~~~

Hysteria billowed behind Abigale's eyes, turning them huge and full of fear. She couldn't quite comprehend what she'd seen. In disbelief she stared back at James or who she thought was James. His eyes! No human ever had eyes that swirled like his. And the thin black slits that centered in his depths, nay not human at all. Animalistic, most definitely. Her hand shook over her mouth to stifle a scream that was lodged in her throat. She shook her head in disbelief.

"Abigale, let me explain." James took a slow step toward her.

Abigale backed away from him, "Don't come near me." Her words were barely a shaken whisper.

Abigale needed to find a way to escape. *What type of monster is the Black Douglas?* she thought and what was he going to do with her? No more was her sense common. There was a beast standing right in front of her waiting for a good chase. Looking over her shoulder she saw the twin wooded doors leading to the outside bailey just a few feet away. Could she make it to those doors and escape before he caught her? She turned back around and met his amber glare and a shiver raced up her spine sending her straight into flight instinct. Fear took over as she dashed through the great hall and out the door.

Relieved to see that Fergus was still in the bailey waiting for the stable groom, with much haste she grabbed the leather reins and hoisted herself up onto him. Taking off in a full gallop toward the forest, she didn't know where she was going. All she knew was that she needed to be far away from Black Stone and that monster.

Chapter 16

Until we meet again…

Hooves thundered through the forest disturbing a flock of black birds sending them up into the gray cloudy sky. Abigale's heart raced faster and faster with each stride Fergus took. Scrapes streaked her skin as low-lying tree branches whipped at her face. She maneuvered her steed, zigzagging between heavily rooted trees when the hem of her dress caught on a branch and ripped a chunk off. She knew she was pushing Fergus faster than she should, but fear had grabbed a hold of the reins and drove her forward. The quicker she was far away from Black Stone, the better she would be.

Those eyes… swirling amber with evil sinister snake-like slits, continued to play in her mind, causing her to look over her shoulder, paranoid that the Bogeyman followed closely behind.

Abigale turned back around and focused intently on getting through the glen. There was a clearing up ahead, not too far. Perhaps there would be a village or town nearby that she could lie low in until she figured out what to do.

It all happened so fast when Fergus stumbled over a root. Before Abigale could catch her balance, she was thrown to the ground. A rock bit into her ribs as she landed on her stomach. The dampness of the forest floor chilled her to the bone as she saw her beloved horse tumble to the ground right before her eyes. She heard the air escape from his lungs. A loud agonized groan echoed through the forest.

Rolling to her side, Abigale clutched her ribs and winced as pain stung her body. When she lifted her auburn head, now full of dry, dead leaves, she saw Fergus lying a few feet away snorting and groaning.

"Nay… Nay…" Abigale stumbled to her feet and slowly walked toward her friend.

As she got closer to him she noticed that an unforgiving unearthed root had wrapped around Fergus's hind leg. He tried to move but he couldn't; his leg was stuck. Abigale fell to her knees next to his head and sobbed uncontrollably. Fergus nickered low and deep as she picked his head up and laid it on her lap. "Nay, Fergus. Ye have to get up," she begged with tears trickling down her cheeks. "Ye have to get up."

~~~~~

James ran through the great hall like a bat straight out of hell, bursting through the double wooden doors toward the stables. Hopping up on his mount, he kicked his mare into a full gallop and took off toward the glen. The need to find Abigale and make her understand he wasn't a beast, drove him with commanding force. Damn him for a fool! Why hadn't he just walked away like he had planned to do? Why had he allowed rage to overcome him? Why had he lost control?

"Marcus," he growled. "He's a dead man."

James rode his black mare with God speed following Abigale's trail through the woods. A blue piece of material clung to a branch. James stopped briefly and took the fabric in his hands. *Abigale.* He was right on her trail.

When he finally reached her, the sight before him shattered his heart into a million pieces. Abigale sat next to Fergus, sobbing. He jumped off his horse and proceeded with caution. He desperately wanted to go to her, wrap her in his arms and take away the sorrow he'd caused her. She was frightened and she looked as though she was hurt.

James moved closer to Abigale, yet still keeping some distance between them. "Lass, we need to talk."

Abigale snapped her head up and froze, her body tensed. He'd found her. Slowly she released her dirk from her thigh and stood. With the dagger in her shaking hand, she pressed it to her slender neck. "Stay away or I'll cut my throat," she demanded.

James put his hands up in surrender. "Abigale, I will no hurt ye. Please put the dirk down," he pleaded and stepped closer. Was she that frightened of him that she was willing to cut her own throat?

Taking a steady step backwards, she pressed the cold metal into her neck until blood was trickling down her skin. She'd meant what she said.

"God's wounds lass! Put the dirk down and let me explain." James began to panic; she was serious. His *bel ange* was beyond afraid; one wrong move and he would be to blame for his wife's death. He'd better tread softly.

"Go on then... explain yerself."

Her eyes were wide, never leaving their focus on him. He saw her pulse jumping in her neck and her chest rapidly moved in and out trying desperately to take in much-needed air. How could he have done this to her? James rubbed a hand over his chest, for it began to tighten and ache. Now was the time to come clean and tell Abigale everything, for he knew he'd already lost her. He could see it in her eyes, he could feel it.

"Not until ye drop the dirk."

Apprehensively, she lowered the bloodstained blade, yet her grip stayed tight.

"I'm Dragonkine. I can shift into a dragon." He paused. "I'm one of the seven Guardians of Scotland." He didn't know how much detail to tell. This wee bit of new information was a lot to comprehend.

Her voice shook with fear. "Dragon. Is that why yer eyes changed?"

148

"Aye."

"Why that's impossible," shaking her head, "dragons dinnae exist."

Genuinely James said, "Ye saw my eyes lass. There's much more to me than that."

"How? I dinnae understand."

James took a deep breath; she deserved the truth. "Aye Abigale, dragons have existed from the beginning of time. Dragons and humans coexisted until there came a time where balance was needed. Our Elders of long ago placed our Dragonkine ancestors here to keep balance between dragons and humans."

Her dark brows furrowed. "Then why aren't there more of yer... kind?"

James took a step closer and was relieved when Abigale didn't move. "'Tis a long story, but our people were brutally massacred by King MacAlpin. Some would say oot of greed." He shrugged his shoulders. "Some would say oot of hate. He showed mercy and saved seven of our warriors, but with it came a hefty price. We agreed to surrender our race to the kings of Scotland."

Abigale fell silent, yet listened intently.

"The fact remains, Abigale, I'm an immortal. I will roam this Earth until someone takes my head. I'm dragon, a fierce beast that's full of hate. And I'm every bit human."

James took another step closer until he was standing right in front of her. He stroked her face with the back of his knuckles and looked deeply into her eyes. "I've tried to shelter ye from all this, Abigale, I swear it. But I can no any longer."

Abigale dropped her dirk as she lost herself in his swirling amber depths. "An immortal? How old are ye?"

James ran his fingers through her hair, picking away the dead leaves. "I'm the youngest out of the seven. I am as old as ye see me now, twenty and eight. I became Dragonkine when my da died."

"So ye are born Dragon... kine."

"Nay, we are chosen by Scottish kings and dragon elders. My da happened to be the strongest warrior Guardian so when he died I took his place."

"Does my father know," Abigale paused and swallowed hard, "ye're a dragon?"

"Aye. I believe that's why he wanted me to marry ye. To keep ye safe." Up until this moment, James had never been so thankful and honored to be married to King Robert's daughter. If only he hadn't been such a fool.

~~~~~

Abigale's head was spinning out of control. All the rumored tales of the Bogeyman were true. James was a monster, a beast... a dragon. She shook her head in disbelief. She had so many questions to ask, but couldn't form a coherent thought. *Dragonkine... Immortal.* He was endless, time didn't exist in his world. How... how was her future with James going to compare to her mortal life? He would watch her grow old as he stayed young.

At that time a groan and heavy snort broke through Abigale's thoughts. James and Abigale looked over at Fergus as he lay on the forest floor. Without hesitation, Abigale ran over to him and dropped to her knees. "Nay... Fergus, get up."

James crouched down and examined the fallen steed. It didn't look good, not at all. His hind leg was mangled and twisted deep within a root. Having seen this happen many times, especially on the battlefield, James knew Fergus wasn't going to make it. James continued his examination until he saw a sharp branch embedded in the stallion's chest. Not a good sign.

James stood and raked a hand down his face. "Abigale, I'm sorry, but Fergus isn't going to make it."

"Nay, he'll be fine once we get him back home." Denial had set in, giving Abigale false hope. She couldn't lose Fergus, nor was she going to leave the glen without her friend. He had to get up… he just had to.

"I'm sorry lass, but if we remove that branch the stress alone will kill him." James pointed to the bloody branch. "The only kind thing we can do for him is to put him out of his misery."

"Nay!" Abigale cried out. She sobbed uncontrollably as she ran her hands through Fergus's white and gray mane. "No, Fergus."

She'd seen the blood. Heck, she'd even seen the branch protruding from his chest, but she refused to believe Fergus was dying. She noticed the labored breathing and that his eyes were wide, indicating he was in a tremendous amount of pain. He was indeed suffering.

James crouched down by Abigale and took her tear-streaked face in his hands. With great compassion, he wiped a tear from her cheek. "Ye cannae let him suffer. Let me help him," James pleaded with her.

Her world stood still; sound muted, movement stilled, and Abigale went numb. His words were understood; Fergus suffered, yet she couldn't respond. She had to make the dreadful decision to end his misery and she had never felt so helpless. A surgeon mended wounds and healed the sick, but her expertise and experience couldn't save her friend. Eight years was too short. He deserved more time. It wasn't fair.

Abigale nodded her head, accepting Fergus's fate. She leaned over Fergus and whispered in his ear, "Be brave my friend. I'll see ye soon." Abigale slowly stood, never taking her eyes off of her beloved. She began to walk toward a clearing in the forest just a few feet away, allowing James to do the honorable thing.

As Abigale reached the clearing, every raw emotion she was holding back slammed into her like rushing waves crashing into sand; repeatedly, wave after wave pounded her as if she was stuck in a riptide trying to swim against its turbulent current. She could no longer tread the sea of sorrow and make it back to shore. Abigale broke down and fell to her knees wrapping her arms around her stomach. No matter how hard she hugged herself, she couldn't stop shaking. Tears streamed down her cheeks and disappeared as they hit the forest floor. "Why Fergus… why?" she sobbed.

~~~~~

The sight of Abigale on her knees rocking back and forth, crying, was absolute torture. He wished he could take her pain away. He wished he'd stopped her before she ran out of Black Stone. Why was it that every time he was around, he caused her so much pain, when all he really wanted all along was to love her?

James walked over to Abigale and placed a hand on her shoulder and squeezed. He wasn't a man of many words and didn't know what to say, but he wanted her to know he was here for her.

"Dinnae touch me," Abigale sneered. She stood and faced him. "Don't ever touch me again." Her blue eyes pierced him. "This is yer fault and I will never forgive ye." Tiny fists pounded at his chest. His pectorals flinched, absorbing every blow as he allowed her to lash out her anger.

"I mean it, James Douglas, I curse the day I ever set eyes on ye," Abigale cried.

James wrapped his massive arms around her. Giving her his strength was all he could do, for no words of wisdom or comfort could take the hurt away. He pulled her tight against his chest. She struggled against his hold but the more she fought, the tighter he held her. He would hold her until there was no fight left, until she wept her last tear.

Before long, Abigale gave up and her body went limp in his arms. James picked her up and whistled for his mare. The black warhorse came at once. Once mounted, James sat behind Abigale cradling her across his lap as they left the glen to return to Black Stone. As soon as they were settled, he would send a group of men to retrieve Fergus and make sure he was given a proper burial.

Chapter 17

Without darkness your true light can not be tested.

Off in the distance, dark graying clouds gathered high above, creeping across the light blue sky. The wind picked up and blew angry ripples across the deep blue water of the loch. James sat on a boulder looking toward the brewing storm slowly approaching. The wind blew again, but this time there was a slight chill in the air causing his skin to prickle. *"I curse the day I met ye, James Douglas,"* whispered through the breeze. He shifted his body and pulled his cloak up around his shoulders. Aye, a storm was coming.

Back to the task at hand, he extended a black claw and began to carve into a piece of birch. He'd been here since the mist rose and would stay until the storm threatened to unleash its wrath.

Two days had passed since that dreadful day, yet Abigale was still mourning the loss of Fergus. She refused to get out of bed, refused to eat, and refused everyone except Alice and Effie. Then again the girls were overly protective of her and didn't allow visitors, though they couldn't prevent the laird from sleeping outside her bedchamber door every night. James didn't take no for an answer when it came to Abigale's safety. If someone was out there wanting to harm his *bel ange*, they would have to go through him first.

His cherished deerhound Lennox's ears perked up, and she stood as if to alert him that someone was approaching. "Easy lassie," James reassured her. He already knew who it was. Dragons knew their own kind.

"I thought I'd see ye out here." Conall bent down and patted Lennox on her head.

"Aye, Conall, I was expecting ye." James continued to whittle.

Standing next to James with his arms crossed over his chest, he looked straight ahead at the deep blue loch. "She's beautiful… isn't she?"

"Aye."

They stood in uncomfortable silence for a moment. Conall had something on his mind, yet he proceeded to take his time. Conall shifted his eyes to the ground and rocked back on his heels. "I come to ask for yer forgiveness, my Laird."

James creased his brows. "For what?"

"For leaving ye on the trail alone. 'Tis my fault ye were--"

"Conall, I was an arse to ye. I dinnae blame ye for leaving."

Conall exhaled in relief. Most men would have found their heads on spikes for leaving their laird unprotected, but they had a different type of relationship. They were close like brothers and quite frankly James was the only one Conall truly trusted.

Needing to know more about the attack on his friend, he took a deep breath and questioned him. "Do ye think the shooting and the raid were led by the same person?"

"I dinnae know, but it seems to me someone wants my attention. I believe they raided the village looking for Abigale. It was not by luck. They knew she would be in the village."

"Have you talked with Magnus about the attacks?"

"Aye, he feels that there's a change in the atmosphere and the Earth has become unbalanced." James struck his claw against the birch in aggravation. "And there's a weed in the garden that needs to be pulled."

Conall smirked and shook his head. "I really wish the old man didnae speak in riddles."

"He's requesting an audience with the dragon elders."

"How is he going to do that?" Conall questioned.

James looked up from his carving and asked himself the same question. This would not be an easy task. It would require Magnus to travel to a realm beyond their world. A realm where dragons ruled. Knowing the dangers that lay ahead, James knew that there was more to it than just an attack. Indeed the Earth was beginning to shift. "I dunno my friend, but Magnus can be verra convincing."

"A traitor," Conall growled.

"Aye."

"Why betray your own kind?" Conall shook his head in disgust. Loyalty was something dragons took very seriously. Loyalty meant you were family, and family didn't turn to the enemy side and live to tell the tale.

Blowing the birch dust away from his creation, James paused and looked over the loch as if he was searching for answers. "We are all made of greed, Conall. No matter how much power, coin, or battles won we'll always want more."

"James, ye make us sound like English filth. We are nothing like them."

"And how so?"

"We protect our Scotland and they want to destroy her. As long as I have my head attached and a breath in my body I will fight to defend her."

"I once believed that too, my friend, but too much innocent blood has been spilled." A thought of Abigale, who was innocent, came to mind. She was born into danger just because of who her father was, and now because of him, she was in more danger. He was betting his life on it, someone knew he was a dragon, and what better way to kill a dragon than to steal his mate, or even worst kill his mate?

"Have ye been to see Abigale?"

Conall had to ask, didn't he? A black claw scraped against the wood as James continued to carve. "Nay, Alice and Effie have made it perfectly clear that Abigale is in no mood to be graced by my presence." He said it half jesting.

Conall chuckled. "Och, why don't ye let me take care of the lassies?" He devilishly winked.

For some reason James knew there was more to it than just distracting the girls so he could see Abigale. There was a bonny, free spirited redhead that had his attention.

"Conall, yer a good man. I'll be back to Black Stone shortly."

With that being said, Conall nodded his head and turned on his heel, but before he left, he turned back around to his friend. "I've had my share of darkness, but I chose to open the door and let the light shine in." With nothing more spoken, he hopped up on his chestnut mount and headed back to Black Stone with a special woman on his mind.

James watched Conall as he rode off. Pondering his words of wisdom for a moment, he wondered if it was too late for him. He'd unlocked his door, even if it was only a crack. Now it was Abigale who was shutting the door. He never meant to hurt her, but here he was trying to gather up his courage to ask for her forgiveness. For the first time in his life he realized just how out of control he'd become. Conall was right; he needed Abigale. She calmed him in ways that he had a hard time explaining. She was comfort to his despair and had rekindled his light. No more did he

want to live with the darkness inside of him. He wanted to be the man...
the dragon she deserved.

On the other hand, he knew he had to let her go, if she wanted to
leave. Frankly, why would she want to stay after what he'd put her
through? Aye, she deserved better. There was one last chance to make it
right, then whatever the outcome, maybe he would accept it and move
on.

Retracting his black claw back into his fingertip, James held the
carving up toward the last bit of remaining sun before the rain fell. He
examined his work; nice smooth edges and intricate details were whittled
to perfection. He slipped the tiny treasure into the inner pocket of his
jerkin. James stood up and walked to his black mare as Lennox followed
right behind him. It was time he faced Abigale, whether she wanted to
see him or not.

Chapter 18

When playing with a fire dragon; be prepared to feel the burn.

James paced outside of Abigale's bedchamber practicing over and over in his head what he was going to say to her. On his way back to Black Stone, he'd thought about how Abigale was going to react to him. He ran through worst and best case scenarios, yet it was the former one that he dreaded the most.

What if Abigale threw his arse out or worst threw something at him? What if she wouldn't listen to him as he poured his heart out? Better yet, mayhap she would forgive him and he could spend the rest of his days making his wife scream his name. Nay, that was as farfetched an idea as to say brownies secretly lived in the castle, using their magic to clean. Now wouldn't Alice like a few of those creatures scouring about?

James was procrastinating. He scrubbed a hand down his face. "God's blood." Wasn't he a warrior who had planned out numerous strategic battle tactics, commanded many men to victory, and fought back to reclaim his lands? Instead here he stood scared to death, trembling like a wee child. Like the wee child he'd been the day when he was forced to leave his father and his whole world was forever changed. James's chest tightened and he clenched his jaw.

Enough time had been wasted, he was going into that bedchamber, right words or not.

Softly, James tapped on the door, only to be welcomed with silence. Without a doubt, she was in there; a soft sigh and the rustle of blankets gave her away.

James opened the door, but didn't cross the threshold. In front of him on his large billowing bed, nestled underneath the sheets, Abigale lay. A black silk canopy lined with red Celtic knotwork hung over the bed and was parted on either side. The hearth warmed the room and cast an orange glow, dimly illuminating the dark room. As he entered the chamber a tang smell assaulted his senses. *Sage.* Aye, Alice was up to her cleansing rituals. He inwardly laughed at the thought of Alice smudging the room of evil spirits as he freely walked toward Abigale. How ironic.

Standing by the foot of the bed, James's heart pounded against his ribcage when he saw Abigale lying on her side. Linen sheets molded to her body revealing her supple curves, auburn curls splayed over her shoulder, and her breasts were barely hidden under her night dress, giving him a flawless view. His cock hardened reminding him just how much he wanted to be buried deep inside her. Her beauty had always had this effect on him, arousing him until he went daft.

Reaching out, James touched her foot and began to recall his well thought out apology. He cleared his throat and swallowed down the bile that began to rise up from his stomach. "Abigale, I---"

Abigale turned over onto her back and pinned him with a cold emotionless gaze, yet her eyes shone sorrowfully. Every word and phrase escaped him, leaving him speechless, every well thought out scenario went black, and every bit of bravery left him. Expressing himself seemed pointless now when it was obvious she still hated him.

There were no tears, nor an angered crinkle across her forehead. At the very least, he'd expected that reaction. A coldness he'd never seen in her before left him chilled to the marrow. And knowing he did this to her left him full of regret.

James squeezed her foot tenderly as if his touch could bring her some kind of comfort. Abigale drew her foot away from him and rolled over, turning her back on him, completely shutting him out.

As James was making his way to the head of the bed, two big trunks came into view, causing him to halt suddenly. His heart clenched and deep inside his dragon moaned in sorrow. Abigale had packed for

Bothwell. *She planned on leaving him*, he realized. As if he gave no credence to the wooden chest, he looked at them and then back to Abigale. With this in mind, he understood she was already gone and he was too late.

The room filled with silence except for the hard rain that pelted the window. James walked toward Abigale with only her back to view. Bending down, he took an auburn curl in his hand. He stroked the curl with his thumb. "I've already lost ye, lass, haven't I?" A burning sensation behind his whiskey-colored eyes stung as tears began to collect. He let go of the curl and watched it fall upon her pillow. Abigale didn't move, nor mutter a sound when he touched her. It was time for him to go but he couldn't move, for the fear that leaving her meant he would never see his *bel ange* again.

James stood and reached inside the pocket of his jerkin, pulling out the wooden sculpture he'd made by the loch. Giving it one last look, he placed it on the nightstand by the bed. One last glance at Abigale and then he left the bedchamber.

Once outside the room, James strode away from her and his whole world came crashing down on him. Every word he wanted to say now echoed down his empty corridor mocking him for a bloody coward. Every step he took reminded him that she was moving on, confirming all along he'd been right. He didn't want a wife, but needed Abigale more than he needed the air he breathed.

~~~~~

The force of the door shutting sent a shiver down Abigale's spine and caused her body to jerk. There were no tears left to shed, there were no emotions left to feel. Alice had informed her this morn that two days had passed, but for the life of her she couldn't recall where they had gone. Time had stood still as one day molded into another.

After the emotional numbness wore off from Fergus's death, she came to her senses and blamed herself for his death. James did the honorable thing by putting Fergus out of his misery. She should have never rode him that hard through the glen. It was her fault, but she had had to escape those eyes.

Being that she had some time, Abigale needed to sort through her thoughts. Countless times, she'd questioned her feelings and why she stayed where she wasn't wanted. Had she been so absorbed by to her own dreams and fantasy of having a family that she refused to accept reality? The reality of a man who didn't want her. Why was she holding on white knuckled to a man who was uncontainable? The idea that she could keep a man like James within her bounds was absurd.

If she listened to good reason she would go to Bothwell and begin a new life. After all she still had her freedom. On the contrary if she listened to her heart it would most definitely deceive her.

James was an honorable man, her inner conscience teased her relentlessly. Not once did he take advantage of her. In fact he'd saved her from a night of humiliation and a tarnished reputation. He was dedicated to her father; by marrying her he'd given up his days on the battlefield even though he had no desire to fulfill the king's orders. Through his blunt and abrasive nature he showed her that he cared for her the only way he knew how, she supposed. Surely, anyone who had to deal with a dragon inside of them had their own burdens to bear.

Then as if the clouds had lifted and the sun sprang to life, it dawned on her. The whole entire time, he was protecting her from himself. A dragon. Quickly Abigale sat up in bed. James was a dragon. The more she said it, the more she believed it. Her stomach flopped like a fish trying to swim upstream. She was in love with a dragon.

Nonsense, she scolded. Abigale threw the cover aside and leapt out of bed. Her heart indeed held true to its devious ways.

She paced the small space in front of her window as rain pelted against its glass. *James was here, why didn't he say something?* she mused. *Abigale Bruce, ye didn't give him much of a chance.* Her inner muses were out in full force. She shook her head. "I'm going to Bothwell and far away from… him." Saying it out loud stung a little deeper than she'd expected. "Besides," she folded her arms across her chest, "I won't have to pack." Her trunks had just arrived a few days ago from Castle Douglas and there they sat, unpacked and stacked neatly in the corner.

Abigale quit pacing when she noticed from across the room something standing on her nightstand that wasn't there before. Odd, she normally kept a candle and snuffer and occasionally a book on the table, nothing more. Crossing the room, she walked toward the foreign object. When she got closer, a wooden statuette of a horse stood tall and proud. Taking the figurine into her hands, she smoothed her fingers over the wood and creased its head. "It's Fergus." Bewildered and holding back a few tears, she inspected the steed inch by inch. Every detail whittled into the birch was a testament to Fergus's perfection. Every strand of hair and muscle definition was masterly carved, even down to his hooves.

"James," she whispered.

With the figurine in hand, Abigale raced to the door and down the corridor. She had to find James. Auburn curls bounced with each step she took, bare feet padded on cold stone floors as she opened every bedchamber door in search of the man she loved. What a fool she'd been. He'd come to her and she had turned him away. *Fool.* Continuing her search, she raced down the stairs, through the great hall, and into the kitchen. But James was gone as if he'd vanished. He couldn't be far; he was just in her chamber.

Cold, damp air bit through her light linen night gown. Needless to say it didn't stop her as she stepped back into the great hall. Only stopping to catch her breath, it dawned on her… the solar. He had to be in the solar.

A soft glow of light filtered beneath the solar door. Abigale placed her hands on the cold wooden door, closed her eyes, and prayed he was in there. She gave the door a push and it opened without protest. The room was lit by the raging fire flickering in the hearth. No candles were lit which left the corners of the room dark and eerie. As she open the

163

door further, she could see James sitting in a chair in front of the flames with his elbows resting on his knees and his head in his hands as if he was mourning the loss of a loved one. Her heart ached for him.

To give them some privacy, Abigale shut the door behind her then sauntered over to the hearth. "Thank ye for my gift. 'Tis beautiful." Her voice shook a little on her last word.

Startled, James's head shot up. "Abigale?" He must have been in deep thought, for he'd not heard her enter the room.

Avoiding eye contact, she looked at her trinket meekly. "I'm sorry for blaming ye for Fergus's death. It was wrong of me and I hope ye can forgive me."

"Aye, I forgive ye, but I dinnae blame ye for being upset with me. I should have told ye sooner what I was."

Abigale stood in front of the hearth just a few feet away from James, yet she could feel the heat from his gaze as if he was standing next to her. Her beautiful, wicked Highlander raked his whiskey-colored eyes over her body. The raging flames behind her shone through her night gown leaving nothing to his imagination. Her legs were long and lean, hips were flared, and breasts were begging for his touch.

James cleared his throat. "So, I was wondering when ye plan on leaving for Bothwell?"

What? Abigale was confused. She'd never mentioned to James about leaving for Bothwell. Granted the last time her leaving Black Stone was brought up, she told him she wasn't leaving. It wasn't until recently she'd thought about changing her mind. Oh no. Abigale's throat went dry. *Could dragons read minds? Had James read her mind?*

"I saw that yer trunks were packed and… well…I—"

"Nay." Abigale let out a small chuckle. "My trunks arrived when I was taking care of ye and I hadn't had a chance to unpack." She paused. "Ye thought I was leaving?"

"Aye." James's face seemed to relax a little.

"Well, I would be lying if I said that the thought didnae cross my mind, but nay, James, I dinnae wish to leave."

Abigale could almost see James's shoulders drop with relief knowing that she wasn't leaving. "Good, because I wouldn't be able to let ye go if I tried. So lass, why are ye here then?"

The deepness of his voice smoothed over her body sending cold shivers over her skin. Knowing that he wanted her to stay gave her all the strength and courage she needed. With inches to spare between them, Abigale stopped in front of him and straightened her shoulders. "'Tis like I said before my Laird, I come to thank ye." She arched a brow and smiled.

"My lady, I must warn ye, when ye play with fire, ye get burned." His eyes held a truth to them so she knew he meant every word he said.

Abigale felt herself being pulled toward James until she straddled him. Large hands rested on her hips, and she felt the strength of his grip.

Abigale traced her fingers along his face noticing the coarseness of stubble along his jaw, reminding her that he was pure raw male, while the scar under his right eye reminded her that he was a warrior wielding strength and power, and the softness of his lips reminded her of how soft his heart could be. He purred low and deep, relishing her caress, reminding her he was every bit dragon.

Truly she loved this man with all her heart, even his rough edges and imperfections.

"James, please forgive me for my actions and cruel words. I didnae mean them."

A hooded gaze stared back at her. This close she could see amber waves swirling in his eyes like poured whiskey. "There's nothing to be forgiven."

"But--"

"Shhh. Kiss me." James took Abigale's head in his hands and pulled her into a soft kiss. Needing more of her, he licked at her full lips and intensified the kiss. Her heart raced, sending molten lava through her veins. The fluttering in her stomach was back making her core throb. These new-found feelings were like nothing she had ever felt before, yet she wanted more. Craved more.

A rough but gentle tug of her hair made Abigale's lips break contact. Dominant enough to get Abigale's attention, James held her firmly and gazed deeply into the blueness of her eyes. "Do ye love him?" A shadow of the menacing Black Douglas lingered across his face as he waited for her to answer.

"Who?" Confusion crossed her face.

James tightened his grip on her hair as the name passed over his lips. "Marcus."

Abigale brought her hands up and covered his, loosening his grip. She whispered over his lips, "I'm here with ye, James Douglas." She took his bottom lip into her mouth and sucked before claiming his mouth.

Strong arms circled her tiny body pulling her even closer. She slipped her hands over his broad shoulders and down his back until she reached the hem of his tunic then lifted it over his head, throwing it to the stone floor.

Soft lips kissed down the tender part of her neck just below her ear leaving a blazing trail of heat behind. James yanked down her night gown. The coarseness of his massive hands tenderly squeezing her breasts drove her daft and just when she had thought the torture would stop, he traced small circles around her peaked nipples turning those fluttering butterflies into flames.

Continuing his delicious assault on her breasts, he took a pink nipple in his mouth and sucked until Abigale moaned her pleasure. Wanting more, she threw her head back, giving him complete access to her body; it was his to command. She desired more of his wickedness as he kissed, licked, and sucked her peachy skin.

Feeling an intensity billowing deep within her core, Abigale rocked her hips forward to relieve the ache. A soul-shaking feral growl rumbled through James and before Abigale could react her night dress was ripped clean off her body and lay in a torn heap on the floor. A rush of cold air pricked her skin which only strengthened the sensation. What was this man doing to her?

James pulled her closer, and their hot bare skin touched, igniting a fire that set them ablaze. She wondered if he could feel how she burned for him, even though he still wore his kilt. As she rocked her hips, James hissed and grabbed her arse and rubbed her sex against his cock. Abigale threw her hands into his long black hair when he took her nipple into his mouth and nipped. A wave of heat spiraled through her body. Aye, Sister Kate was right… Highlanders were a wicked breed.

"James," Abigale moaned breathlessly, "what are ye doing to me?"

"Och lass, do ye trust me?"

She nodded. James slipped his hand between her legs and gently stroked her virginal nub. With hands that had mastered pleasuring a woman in every way, he gently slipped his finger deep inside of her, careful not to hurt her. Abigale sucked in a shaky breath.

James looked up at her. "Did I hurt ye?"

"Nay and don't ye dare stop," Abigale commanded.

James was more than happy to oblige.

James pulled his finger out only to plunge it in further and faster until Abigale felt her walls tightening. By all means, he was taking her down a path she'd never traveled, furthermore creating a carnal necessity that drove her further and faster to a destination that led her straight to bliss. As if he knew exactly what to do and the exact time to do it, he slipped in a second finger. Abigale sighed in pure pleasure, she held on tight, wrapping her arms around his neck. Surely if she let go she would crash and break into a million pieces.

"Look at me, lass," James whispered.

Abigale shook her head no. Her insecurity had crept up on her. Never being with a man before she couldn't help but feel inadequate when it came to pleasing him.

A strong hand pulled the back of her neck, bringing her head down so their foreheads touched. "Look at me, my *bel ange*."

Abigale opened her eyes to the most breathtaking man she'd ever seen.

A man of raw power.

A man of honor.

A man that was a dragon.

A man that did wicked things to her body that she craved. She found a strength in his eyes that made the world fade away.

"I want to see you shatter, lass," James whispered against her lips.

As if it was a command, a wave of warmth tingled through her body as Abigale's walls came crashing down and she indeed shattered into a million delicious pieces. "By the saints," she moaned and threw her arms around James's neck as another wave of heat hit her.

For a moment they held each other tightly as she caught her breath.

"I'm not done with ye, lass," James whispered in her ear.

Abigale snaked her hands down his neck and grazed the thickness of his chest. "Just what do ye plan to do to me?" she teased.

His eyes never leaving hers, he unbuckled his leather belt. Black fabric unfolded and fell to the side revealing his hardened length.

Abigale watched every move he made. She was curious and wanted to explore every inch of his sinful body, yet her eyes grew wide when she saw what lay between them. At half-mast the tip of his length reached his navel. Abigale arched a questioning brow and looked at James who was quite amused by her astonished reaction.

"Dinnae worry," he smiled and reassured, "we'll take it slow."

Abigale licked her lips and swallowed. "I trust ye."

~~~~~

James took great pleasure in the sight before him; flawless peachy skin with red blotches from his kisses covered her chest and neck. Indeed these were his markings and he intended to leave more. His *bel ange*. Knowing he breached unchartered territory, he was determined to make sure that Abigale's first time was going to be beyond anything she had ever experienced. He would take it slow and sweet until she was ready for him.

James kissed her hard before he stood her up so that she straddled his length. As she stood, two perfectly round breasts were at eye level begging for his touch. He leaned in and sucked on a nipple. Gently,

James positioned himself at her opening and rubbed the tip of his length back and forth, letting her familiarize herself with the feel of him. *God's Blood,* her slick wet heat drove him with fierce need.

Slowly he entered the tip of his cock inside her. Abigale tensed and grabbed hold of his shoulders. He paused for a moment. "Relax love." He smoothed his free hand down her thigh trying to relax her. It must have worked; of her own accord she slid down his shaft slowly inch by inch.

James felt the smoothness of her breasts on his chest as she slid further down. He shuddered. He'd better start counting cows… fast, for he didn't know how much of this sweet torture he could take. The urge to thrust deep inside her and stake his claim kindled to a roaring flame.

They were getting close to the point where he knew it would be uncomfortable for Abigale. Virginity was a precious gift she was giving him, yet he would have to hurt her in order to receive it. James gripped Abigale's hips and stopped before he reached her maidenhood.

Abigale took his face in her hands. "Don't ye dare, James Douglas, I want all of ye."

With one hard thrust he broke through her maidenhood and buried himself to the hilt. With each push he felt Abigale stretch as he filled her more and more. James felt his release building and grabbed her arse pushing her toward her own release. Abigale threw her head back and succumbed to the pleasures James brought out of her. "Oh God, James Douglas," she screamed.

His name echoed throughout the solar and straight to his cock, as with one final earth-shattering thrust he spilled his seed deep inside her.

James would have never thought that surrendering to anyone would feel so sweet, but as they sat there for a moment completely content, wrapped up in each other's arms, James knew he would surrender to Abigale time and time again. His *bel ange.* No doubt about it, his beautiful wife was made for love making. Passion shone through her deep blue eyes when she had shattered beneath his hands and he hoped he would see it again… soon.

Abigale rested her head on top of James's head as he trailed his hands up and down her back. "Did I hurt ye?"

James was concerned because Abigale hadn't said a word nor moved. Being this was her first time, he didn't know how she would react after the deed was done. Abigale lifted her head and smiled a wicked grin. "Can we do that again?"

James cupped her face with his massive hands and smiled a sexy grin. "Aye, at least two more times tonight and then again in the morn." He kissed her. With their bodies still connected, he began to stand. Abigale wrapped her arms around his neck and her legs around his waist.

"Then again after we break our fast." Again he kissed her as he walked towards a brown bear-skin rug lying by the hearth. "Then again at midday." Another kiss as he laid her down on the furry rug. "And how aboot sunset?" James wiggled his eyebrows before he trailed hot blazing kisses down her neck. Abigale giggled, "My Laird, I won't be leaving our bedchamber."

"That's the plan, lass."

Chapter 19

He was immortal; he was never ending.

Fully sated after another round of love making, James rested his head on Abigale's chest, holding her tight as their naked, sweat-covered bodies glistened by the hearth. Silence fell between them. The only sound was the crackling of the fire. Abigale stared into the flickering flames, deep in thought. Strand by strand, she combed through James's hair with her fingertips, letting the long black locks fall upon her breasts.

Questions lingered in her mind about dragons. Dragons? Never would she have believed such nonsense, but she saw the swirls in his eyes right in front of her. There was no denying it, which left her mind consumed with one particular question. Could they have children?

Another thought crossed her mind that gave her a mental shake. Magic? Aye, there was something magical about her wicked Highlander. There had to be some kind of magic pumping in his body, for no flesh and blood human had his capability of abnormal healing abilities. Then there was the memory loss she had experienced. Two full days were left unaccounted for and it still bothered her that she couldn't remember how she arrived at Black Stone.

Instantly her body ignited as James ran his thumb over one of her nipples, sending a shiver down her spine. Indeed dragons possessed magic. She closed her eyes and inwardly sighed.

"What's going on in that beautiful head of yers, *bel ange*? Ye seem far away." James kissed the top of her breast and trailed another kiss to her neck.

"'Tis nothing."

James halted his relentless attack on her neck and held her gaze with stern demanding amber eyes. "Lass, one thing I can no tolerate is lies. Tell me what troubles ye. Ask me anything, love and I'll answer it."

Not wanting to know the answers about children quite yet, Abigale fumbled through what she was going to say. Dragon talk seemed outlandish, nothing more than a fairy tale.

"Well... do ye... I mean... dragon..."Abigale let out a frustrated breath; she couldn't form a coherent thought.

"Ye mean to ask me if I have magical powers."

"Aye."

"Since I'm immortal, I have the ability to heal myself and I can heal others as well through a deep sleep."

Perking up at his last words, Abigale sat up, resting her weight on her elbows. "I knew it. Ye healed my saddle wounds. That's why I can no remember how I arrived at Black Stone."

"Aye, and before ye ask, aye, I spit fire." James said sarcastically as he lay on his side stretched out on the fur rug facing Abigale. The flames from the hearth backlit her profile casting a golden glow over her skin.

Abigale giggled.

Rolling over to face James, she traced her finger over the scar under his right eye. Indeed he must be a magnificent dragon. It thrilled her, but on the other hand it scared her to know that a beast of a dragon lived deep inside her husband. Could she accept that fact? The dragon was a part of James and she knew without a doubt she loved him, but getting used to a dragon would take some time.

Taking her hand in his, he kissed her palm. "What else ails ye?"

"I can no imagine how painful it must be to know ye'll outlive yer loved ones. Eternity is an awful long time to live."

James rolled over on his back, forearm behind his head. He pulled Abigale tightly by his side. She fit perfectly.

"And ye'll have to watch me grow old and gray." She frowned and took a deep breath before she asked the next question. "And what aboot our children, James? Will they be immortal?"

"Abigale, as long as I'm alive ye will be immortal, but our children will not, unless one of our sons is chosen to become a guardian. I'm sorry." He held onto her tightly. "I know how much ye desire a family. This is why Dragonkine do no marry, because of their immortality."

Their children would be mortal? Abigale fell silent as she wondered if she could endure watching their children grow old while they stayed exactly the same age, or painfully watch their children suffer from sicknesses or worst yet death. She didn't know what to think.

"Abigale, I understand if ye need some time to think this through, but know one thing… I would rather live my immortal life to the fullest with ye and our future children than spend my endless days without ye. I know now, I need ye, lass."

Abigale's heart plummeted to her stomach. He wanted a family… he needed her. She understood exactly what James was saying, to live yer life to the fullest, and she could do that as long as James was by her side.

Rolling on to her stomach, she looked down at James. "So, there's a possibility of wee bairns in the near future?"

He exhaled like he was holding his breath waiting for her to speak. "Aye, as many as ye want." James smirked with the devil in his eyes.

"Well, James Douglas, the man who never wanted a wife," she mocked. "Seems like ye'll have one for a very long time." Abigale smiled and teased his chest with her fingertips.

~~~~~

James returned her smile and kissed her. Indeed he had a bonny lass for a wife and took great pride in knowing he could give her the one thing her heart desired. Children.

James broke their kiss. "There's one more issue to discuss. Marcus. Promise me ye'll stay away from him," James stated bluntly.

"James, he has been a friend to me. Ye have my heart." Abigale bent down to kiss him but was stopped. James stared intently into her eyes. "Promise me."

"I promise. But there's one condition." Now it was Abigale's turn to make her request. "I want the girls to stay here, with us until their parents come for them."

James grumbled his agreement. He would agree to her terms if it meant she would stay far away from Marcus.

"Good." James relaxed his hands and gave her the kiss she wanted. "And I dinnae want ye to leave Black Stone." Slipping that one tiny request in could do no harm.

"James—"

"This is not negotiable," he demanded. There was an enemy close at hand who made no qualms about wanting his attention. It drove him mad that he wasn't any closer to knowing who lurked in the shadows waiting to strike. Hopefully Magnus could obtain some insight from the dragon elders. That was if he was granted an audience. In the meantime, Black Stone was to be heavily guarded and he would make damn sure he protected Abigale with his life.

Abigale rolled her eyes in defeat.

"My lady? Did ye roll your eyes at me?" James teased her as if he was shocked at her reaction. "Do ye understand the punishment for such a display of rudeness?"

Abigale lowered her gaze like she was being scolded, but her grin told a different story. "Nay, my Laird."

In one fluid motion, James pulled Abigale on top of him and covered her arse with his massive hands. Each cheek fit perfectly in his hands and he squeezed. "Punishable by spanking." James wiggled his black brows.

James rubbed her arse cheeks. "I shall take my punishment willfully," Abigale whispered in his ear.

A large hand came down, across both cheeks. The sound of the swat echoed throughout the room. Flames threatened to engulf him as he dealt another smack. With each skin-stinging strike he felt Abigale's arousal.

Pushing her over onto her back, pure raw animalistic power took over. He paused for the briefest moment, before he took her again, and gazed down into her deep blue eyes. "My *bel ange.*"

Chapter 20

In shallow holes moles make fools of dragons. ~ *Chinese Proverb*

If it wasn't for James having to deal with an urgent matter at hand, Abigale would still be in the solar naked and wrapped up in his massive arms. Being the Chief of Clan Douglas of Angus, and a dragon, business needed to be tended to, which gave Abigale time to check on the girls. She was hopeful that the girls would be eager to play outside since the rains had stopped and the sun was shining. The promise of a beautiful morn stood firm.

Abigale winced when she bent down to slip on her winter shoes, reminding her how deliciously sore her body had become after her night with James. A bright smile crossed her face as she stood and smoothed out her hunter green dress with gold trim. The square neckline was high enough to keep her warm, but still showed off her peachy skin. Long flowing sleeves covered her slender arms and opened wide at the ends. As she adjusted the gold knotted sash around her hips, she placed her hands on her stomach. She smiled. Just the thought of one day having a child of her own with the man she loved warmed her heart.

Indeed it was going to be a beautiful morn.

A knock on the door interrupted her day dream when Alice brought the girls into her bedchamber. "My lady, ye look stunning this morn," Alice beamed.

"Thank ye kindly, Alice."

The eldest girl with soft blond hair approached Abigale and bowed. "Good morn, my lady."

Abigale smiled at the child. "Good morn."

The eldest girl had been pleasant, but Abigale sensed the girl didn't trust her fully.

It was obvious Alice had spent a great deal of time with the girls. They were clean, hair perfectly plaited, and dressed in long-sleeved brown wool dresses perfect for playing outdoors. The youngest, who had yet to speak, looked adorable in an elegant white bonnet that sat on top of her blonde head and tied around her chin.

Abigale bent down to the wee girl's level and smiled brightly. The little girl peeked out from behind Alice's skirts. The poor child seemed so timid, yet there was courage behind her blue eyes. "Ye know, I have been itching to go outside." Abigale took the girl's tiny hands in hers. "Would ye like to come with me?" Abigale glanced up at the eldest girl and smiled.

The girl returned her smile. "Yes, my lady."

As Abigale looked back to the wee one, dimples winked back at her as the child beamed from ear to ear. Wee one shook her head up and down with so much enthusiasm Abigale thought that the child would jump out of her skin. Abigale picked her up and held her close. Small skinny arms wrapped around her neck and squeezed, as if saying, I've missed you.

They filed out of the bedchamber and into the long corridor. Before long wee one wiggled and fidgeted to be released, so Abigale put her down. The girls skipped in front of her and Alice, laughing and giggling as they made their way through the castle.

Abigale couldn't have been any happier. Seeing the girls like this warmed her heart. She couldn't stop smiling.

"My lady, may I have a word with ye?" Alice asked.

"Of course Alice, ye may speak freely with me. There's no need to be formal." They joined arms and Abigale squeezed Alice close. "But first I must thank ye for taking such good care of me. Ye are a true friend."

"Och lass, ye know I love ye like my own." Alice patted her hand and smiled. "I do have concerns, my lady, about wee one. She hasn't muttered one word since she has arrived and the eldest does no trust easily. She won't tell me her name nor her sisters." Alice pursed her lips together. "I'm afraid the wee one can no speak."

"Alice, the girls need a little time and lots of love. Do no worry, give it some time," Abigale reassured her. "Has there been any word about their parents?"

Deep down Abigale hated to ask, but she knew that there was a possibility of their mum or da returning for the girls. It disgusted her to think that she would have to return the children to live in poverty, furthermore returning them to undeserving parents. How could anyone raise a family in that filth? Nay, she would protect these girls and never allow anyone to hurt them again.

Alice shook her head. "Nay my lady, no a peep."

Abigale couldn't help but feel relieved about the news. "The laird has given me his word that the girls can stay here until they are claimed. Do we have an empty chamber close to mine?"

"Aye, I will have it prepared."

Suddenly the doors to the great hall leading out to the bailey opened wide. Rory and a few burly warriors entered which gave the girls the perfect opportunity to race outdoors.

As they reached the great hall, Alice excused herself to the kitchen and Abigale raced outside behind the girls.

In passing, Rory nodded his greeting as Abigale flew pasted him. "Good morn Rory."

"Aye, 'tis a good morn, my lady." Rory winked.

~~~~~

A blast of cold fresh air hit Abigale's lungs as warm rays heated her body and sheltered her from the cool morn breeze. Days like today would soon be few and far between, for the sting of winter was approaching fast.

No one was milling around the bailey this morn, except maybe a servant or two. The devoted and dearly loved deerhounds, Lennox and her trusted friend Mahboon, came racing across the grounds, almost knocking the girls down.

Abigale called the girls to her. "How about we play hide and seek."

The girls huddled next to Abigale ready to play. "I'll be the seeker and you two go run and hide."

The girls took off running in search of the perfect hiding place. The eldest called over her shoulder. "No peeking!" she squeaked with a giggle.

Abigale finished the countdown. "Ready or no… here I come."

The sound of scampering feet caught Abigale's attention and she started her search in that direction. Old oak trees with perfect nooks and crannies littered the walls surrounding the castle, making for excellent hiding places. Abigale peeked behind an oak when the dogs ran past.

Both dogs barking, they charged past the gatehouse, and ran with God speed into the nearby forest. Abigale grew cautious as she hurried to find the girls. The eldest girl ran from her hiding spot to find Abigale. The girl must have sensed trouble by the way the dogs were reacting.

"There ye are. Where is yer sister?"

"I dinnae know."

Both of them looked at each other as if they both realized why the dogs took off towards the forest.

"She must be in the forest," Abigale said.

Panicked, they both ran from the secured walls and out into the open wilderness of the forest. Barking echoed throughout the glen, making it easy to follow the dogs. Hopeful that Lennox and Mahboon had found the girl, Abigale called out, "Wee one!" Again she called out even though she knew the girl wouldn't answer. At least Abigale's voice might chase away any wild animals that may be a threat. "Wee one! Come out!"

With the eldest girl right on Abigail's heels, they both came to a sudden stop. Marcus was bent down talking to wee one. He stood up as soon as he saw Abigale approach. He grinned and released the child. "Ye should be more careful where ye roam."

Relieved that she had found the girl, yet alarmed to see Marcus, Abigale called out to her. "Wee one, come here lassie." Wee one happily ran to Abigale.

Never taking her eyes off Marcus, Abigale scooped wee one up into her arms, making sure she wasn't hurt.

A gut feeling told Abigale to get the girls and herself back to the safety of Black Stone. Not wanting to scare the girls, Abigale calmed her rattled nerves and took a settling breath. "Girls, get back to the castle and find Alice. Take Lennox and Mahboon with ye. "

Not trusting the situation, the eldest girl hesitated and gazed at Marcus with a suspicious eye. "Is everything alright, Lady Abigale?"

Marcus stepped closer to the girl. "There's nothing to fear, lass, but ye should do as yer told."

Wee one grabbed her sister's hand as they reluctantly followed the dogs back to Black Stone.

"The lasses look good, Abigale. Much better than the last time I saw them," Marcus stated.

Abigale turned her attention back to Marcus. Dark circles surrounded his eyes as if he hadn't slept in days. A red slash lingered over his right eye. He began to walk up next to Abigale but stopped when she took a step back. With his hands on his hips, he shook his head in disbelief. "He's turned ye against me, hasn't he?" It was more of a statement than a question.

Abigale pretended she hadn't heard him. "I'm sure James is out looking for me. I should be heading back." Abigale turned to head back to the castle until a cold rough hand grabbed her arm.

She tried to pull her arm away from his tight grip but he pulled her closer and wasn't letting go. "Release me right now, Marcus." She wriggled beneath his grip.

"Sorry lass, but ye need to come with me."

"If James catches ye near me he will kill ye. Please just let me go. I will nae say a word," Abigale pleaded.

Deep sinister laughter boomed through the forest. Marcus caught his breath long enough to reply, "Lass, he can't kill me even if he wanted to." He chuckled a few more times before he became very serious. "No one is looking for ye and I saw yer husband leave earlier this morn. He can no help ye now."

Panic prickled up her spine. What was Marcus up to? If she stalled a little longer someone would come looking for her. James was gone but

Alice knew where she was. Perhaps the girls would alert a guard or Alice. She knew someone would be searching for her soon.

"Marcus," she said calmly, "Please release me. Ye're hurting my arm."

Marcus studied Abigale's face for a moment, contemplating her request.

"Please," she begged.

"Ye know, there's something in a way that a lass begs that turns me on." He paused. "Kiss me like ye kiss him, Abigale. Want me like ye want him." He nuzzled his nose against her neck and breathed in deeply. "Ye smell verra pretty."

Abigale began to tremble. She closed her eyes and wished he would let her go. At this point, she would make a run for it. It sickened her being this close to him, for she could smell the mead on his breath, warm and stale. A tear slipped down her cheek. Where was James?

Abigale pulled from Marcus's grip, turned around, and looked for a way to escape, but she was cornered by five massive figures dressed in full battle armor. The pure size alone of these men would make a grown man run to his mother and hide in her skirts. They stood around her with their arms folded across their plated chests, helms covered their faces, and evil poured from their pores.

Bile churned in her stomach and rose in her throat. Her eyes grew big and her pupils dilated as the flight or fight response warred inside her. There was no way she could fight off six huge men nor run from them. Hopefully she could talk her way out of this.

"Marcus, what's going on?" She eyed him directly with suspicion.

Marcus pursued his approach on her until he stood over her looking down into her huge eyes. "My sweet Abigale--" He stopped in mid-sentence as if he warred with himself.

183

Before Abigale knew what was happening, Marcus grabbed her waist and threw her over his massive shoulder. Kicking and screaming, Abigale fought hard to escape him, but it was impossible. He was too big and too powerful.

"Put me down!" Abigale screamed and pounded her fists into his back. She wasn't going without a fight. Doing everything in her might to escape, she bit down on his shoulder blade. Marcus grunted in pain and dropped her instantly. She fell on her back onto the hard forest floor.

Scrambling to her feet, she didn't make it far before she was grabbed from behind. Cold steel chilled her body as a massive armored man held a sword across her neck. One wrong move and she was sure as the heather bloomed in summer that the man who held her would slit her throat without hesitation.

Her chest rose and fell rapidly, as Marcus approached her. "Looks like we have a feisty one here." With the unwounded arm he slapped her hard. Stars exploded behind her eyes and her body went limp.

Chapter 21

Capture the princess, slay the dragon.

Heavy eyelids begged to open as throbbing pain slammed through her. Dampness from the ground seeped through her dress and settled deep in her bones. Abigale lay motionless. Trying desperately to open her eyes, she blinked back the fog until slowly iron bars came into view causing her to panic. Faintly, she heard voices arguing in the distance. Where was she?

As she slowly sat up, her surroundings started to spin and so did her stomach. Blood rushed to her face, increasing the throbbing in her cheek. As she tried to swallow she noticed the taste of blood in her mouth. She spat out the blood and wiped the taste away from her lips with the back of her hand. Events were slowly coming back. She remembered being in the woods with Marcus and... then it dawned on her, Marcus had hit her and knocked her unconscious. He had taken her away, but where?

Abigale rose to her feet. Still unsteady, she fell backwards into the cold iron bars. She looked around and realized she had been locked up inside of an enclosure that looked like a bird cage. It was big enough for her to stand and nothing more. A few lit torches were hung on posts sporadically and cast shadows upon the enclosure's fabric. *A tent.* She must be inside a tent, and judging by the glow of the torches it must be night.

Feeling steadier on her feet, Abigale took a few steps to the front of the cage. She grabbed the thick iron bars and gave them a tug, testing their strength. They were solid. Two figures came into view and stood outside near the entrance of the tent. Although she couldn't see them, their shadows indicated that they were men. Abigale strained to listen, trying to recognize the voices. Aye, she did. One of the voices belonged to Marcus but the other voice was unfamiliar.

"Ye promised if I brought ye the princess, my sister would be returned to me. Now where is she?" Marcus said.

"I would watch that tongue of yers. Ye are in no position to be giving orders." Rickert stabbed a finger at Marcus's chest.

Looking at the finger then back at Rickert, Marcus had a grim feeling he had been deceived. "I want to see my sister."

"Sutton," the sheriff called to his trusted second commander.

"Aye, my lord."

Marcus looked at Rickert as he whispered a command to the burly man. As quick as Sutton came, he left to do his lord's bidding.

Placing his hands behind his back, Rickert stood in front of Marcus. "Ye should know who ye're dealing with before ye trust them, fool. I told ye there would be a village raid. All ye had to do was tell us where to find the princess. Seems to me yer cock got the better of ye, aye?"

"I did as you ordered, I brought ye the princess. What more is there?" Marcus was beginning to lose his patience.

"Aye." The foul man stepped closer until his lips were lingering over Marcus's ear. "I want the dragon."

This was the moment Rickert had been waiting for, his revenge on James. Now with Abigale in his grasp, the dragon would soon come and he would get his revenge. Slay the dragon.

Sutton, now with a wooden box in his hand, came marching up. Handing the box over to his lord, he bowed and walked away.

"Did ye really think ye would see yer beloved sister again? Ye're as naive as yer whore of a sister."

Sweat began to bead across Marcus's forehead and his heart thundered in his chest as he looked at the box. *Nay!*

Pure evil laughter belted out from the sheriff. He threw the box at Marcus's feet. "Be proud, she put up one hell of a fight." He then turned and started to walk away.

The box landed with a soul-shaking thud. Its contents spilled out and a bloody heart lay in the dirt.

Marcus bellowed a mournful cry that echoed across the night and dropped to his knees. With shaking hands, he picked up his sister's non-beating heart and placed it back into the box. Her heart, her kind, good-natured, innocent heart. Marcus shook his head. "Nay!"

Primal animalistic instincts suddenly exploded inside of him sending Marcus into a rage. As he stood, slowly he pulled a dirk from his boot. Sinister hooded eyes glared into Rickert's back as if he was mentally crushing the man. "Rickert!"

Rickert turned around only to find himself nose to nose with Marcus. Without flinching, Marcus drove his blade into Rickert's stomach. Wide-eyed he fell to the ground, dead.

A fool no more, Marcus stood over the dead man. He should have known better than to trust an Englishman's word. But did he really have a choice? Nay, he did what he had to do in order to save his sister and now look where it had gotten him. He'd betrayed his clan and he'd failed his sister.

This was James's fault. The bloody bastard cared only about himself, Marcus seethed inside. Wronging the wrong people would be that bastard's downfall. Burning the English garrison to death to reclaim what? His precious land? His family name? It had always been about

James, hadn't it? James created another enemy, but instead of the enemy destroying James, it destroyed Marcus.

Good thing Marcus had a sharp mind for he knew Rickert to be a cheat, a master of trickery. But never fret, he reminded himself. His sister's death would not be for naught. Everything became crystal clear like a cloudless sky. It had been woven into the fibers of his soul; this was what he was destined to do. All along he could hear the dragon cry, yet fate cannot be rushed, he had to wait for his destiny and his destiny would prevail tonight. Risky as it might be, he had a plan; dragon blood would be spilled tonight and a kingdom would rise again.

~~~~~

Abigale's hand flew over her mouth in shock. She had just witnessed Marcus killing a man. Terror ripped through her and frantically she began to pull at the iron bars, praying they would bend. She had to get out of here.

The flaps of the tent flew open as Marcus's body filled the entrance, causing her to step back towards the back of the cage.

Marcus glanced at Abigale and said, "Ye saw me kill him, didn't ye?"

Abigale stood silent. The hard cold tone of his voice chilled her veins.

"Dinnae fash yerself princess, I'm no going to kill ye."

"I need to know why, Marcus." Her voice shook. "Why did ye kill that man?"

"'Tis best ye stay quiet and don't draw attention to yerself."

"Why did ye bring me here? I trusted ye and ye deceived me."

Marcus strode to the cage. "See lass, that's where ye went wrong." He rubbed his hand through his brown curly hair, as he paced back and forth in front of her. "James has made quite a few enemies. I told him so not too long ago." He looked far away as if he was remembering that day. "I'm afraid yer husband's brutal ways have caught up with him."

"I dinnae understand."

Marcus stopped in front of her and grabbed the iron bars, causing her to flinch. "Abigale, that bastard I killed," he paused like he was trying to rein in his anger, "wanted to kill James for the brutal way he massacred his men when yer husband reclaimed Castle Douglas. Ye were the bait to bring James here."

"And ye agreed to bring me here and betray James. Why? Why would ye do such a thing?"

Marcus looked down at the ground and shook his head. "'Tis none of yer business, it's personal now. James will pay for what he has done to me, mark my words, princess."

There was no room in that blasted cage. Like a wild animal trapped, she felt the need to run, but there was nowhere to go. *Capture the Princess... slay the dragon,* she thought. Gradually, she put the puzzle pieces together as she recalled Marcus asking the man about his sister. Marcus had brought her here to be exchanged for his sister, hadn't he? Oh dear God, he knew James would come for her and that's when they would kill him. Fear pricked her skin and settled in the pit of her gut. This was a trap. She faced Marcus, "Ye don't have to do this. James will forgive ye. Maybe he can help get yer sister back."

"My sister? My sister is of no concern to ye or James."

"But I heard ye talking to a man outside." She motioned to the tent entrance. "She was to be returned to ye. Is she in some kind of trouble? It is why I'm here... aye? He's holding yer sister against ye?"

"Abigale, she's—"

"What?"

Marcus said between clenched teeth, "She's dead."

Abigale took a step back. "Nay, did that man—"

"Murder her, aye. James caused her death and he will pay for it." Every word he spoke dripped with hate.

"Ye can no mean it."

"Aye Abigale." He held her stare. "Eye for an eye." He turned and left the tent.

~~~~~

Alice raced through the great hall, her plump bosom bouncing in stride. James had returned, and barely had the time to brace himself, before Alice rushed him. "My Laird," Alice panted. She could barely speak, she was so winded. "Lady Abigale... I've searched everywhere."

Overwhelming terror shot through him. He sensed something was wrong the moment he walked into the great hall. Normally he could feel Abigale even if she wasn't in the room; his dragon knew his mate. He grabbed Alice's shoulders in order to calm her down. "Lass, take a deep breath. Where is Lady Abigale?"

"I... I do no know." Alice started to sob.

"What do ye mean? She was here this morn."

"She never returned from playing with the girls. The eldest mentioned a scary man in the woods."

"A man, in the woods?" Bloody hell, she had promised him she would not leave the castle walls. With his hands on his hips James started to pace. "Are ye sure?"

"Aye."

"How long has she been gone?"

"I'm no sure, my Laird"

James fought back the urge to shake the answers out of her. "Alice, think. I need to know how long?"

Alice couldn't think straight. Everything began to blur.

At that time Conall and Effie entered the great hall. Realizing the commotion, they instantly raced over to James. "James, what's happened?" Conall said.

James released Alice. Effie quickly caught Alice as she collapsed into her arms.

"Conall, find Rory. Abigale is missing," James ordered.

"Aye." Conall was gone as quickly as he arrived.

"Effie, stay here in case Abigale shows up."

"Aye," Effie confirmed.

With haste James stormed up the stairs and toward their bedchamber. Although James knew better than to believe in false hope, he still held on to it as he entered their room. The door slammed open. "Abigale!"

Nothing. No sigh of Abigale anywhere.

James sat down on the bed resting his head in his hands. He shook his head as if wiping away a bad dream. Doubt began to fill his mind; she couldn't be gone. What if she had left of her own free will? Was she having second thoughts about being married to a dragon? That alone was enough to make a lass run. Nay, she wasn't a runner. They would have talked about it; that he knew for sure. Alice mentioned a scary man in the woods. Panic pricked him like a thistle. Someone had taken his woman.

With time being of the essence, James stood up and began to quit the room when something shiny and gray caught his eye sticking out from under the bed. Squinting his eyes to focus, he bent down and picked the object up. It was an arrow head. He turned it around and studied the arrow; his blood stained it. The arrow head was the same one that Abigale had removed from his chest. As he looked closer more information became clear. It was made out of flint. "God's blood," James cried out. Marcus. He was the only one who made his arrow heads out of this kind of flint. The room started to spin as he took in all this information. Marcus had tried to kill him.

Anger like he'd never felt before pulsed through him, and his dragon stirred impatiently waiting to be released. James squeezed the arrow head until blood trickled down his hand. Indeed there was a traitor lurking around clan Douglas and he had just been found out. James cursed and threw the arrow at the stone wall with such force that it became embedded deep within the stone. "I will take the bastard's head."

James stormed out of the room in search of Rory. If anyone could find Abigale, Rory was the one. Out of all the Guardians, his tracking ability was superior. However, James prayed that he wasn't too late.

Chapter 22

Unless a serpent devour a serpent it will not become a dragon. ~ Chinese Proverb

James sat perched on his massive black war horse on top of the cliff looking down into the valley below. The highland winds blew and rattled the nearby trees that concealed their presence. Conall was mounted on his chestnut steed next to James. His horse pranced in anticipation. "If anyone can find Lady Abigale, 'tis Rory."

"Aye." James sat motionless, amber eyes swirling intensely as he searched for movement below. Rory led them right to Marcus, but the campsite was unnervingly quiet. James sent Rory to find Abigale just in case the enemy had moved her to a different location. Even though James could sense that she was here, he wanted to make sure before they attacked.

James noticed movement towards a smaller cliff and nodded in that direction. "At least two hundred archers over there."

Conall observed and concurred, "Aye."

"Och lads, two hundred men and four dragons seems like a disadvantage. Should we play nice?" Magnus said.

"Magnus, if yer lady was held captive… would ye play nice?" James bit back.

"Nay, I'd gut them where they stood."

A rustle nearby turned their bantering to silence as they drew their swords and waited for an attack.

Rory looked like he had just seen the Devil himself. Three swords stared at him with their pointy ends promising to slash his throat. "God's Blood, ye almost made me shite myself!"

James sheathed his sword and waited for Rory to speak. "Well?"

"Lady Abigale is here. See that red tent by the forest tree line?" Rory pointed to the tent. "Yer lady is in there. Alive."

Relieved at the good news, James exhaled. "And Marcus?"

"Aye, he's here. I can feel the bastart." Rory's eyes narrowed in disgust.

Once James had informed his men about Marcus and how he'd betrayed the clan, the Dragonkine warriors were shocked and confused. Marcus was one of only a few humans the warriors allowed in their inner circle; primarily because he was James's cousin. Dragon he was not but he fought on the battlefields like he was. Marcus was considered one of their own. So his betrayal was a bitter brew to swallow.

"Rory, Magnus, stay here and watch those men." James pointed to the small cliff where the archers were posted. "Conall, come with me."

~~~~~

Marcus and the group of five armored men walked through the campsite. After the news of Sheriff Rickert's sudden passing, the men who held true to the late sheriff became unruly. Marcus needed to put an end to it. Either you were with him or against him, there was no in between. It wasn't necessary that they needed Rickert's table scraps of an army. Five inhuman savages could take down an army twice the size without batting an eyelash. Aye, the Creepers came in handy.

With each footstep, Marcus could feel every lash upon his skin due to the sheriff's beatings begin to tingle, and rage bubbled in his veins. "Are the archers positioned?"

The knight bowed his head to confirm.

"Very well." Marcus turned to the five. "Remember the lady is to be unharmed." The leader of the group nodded and drew his sword. No words were spoken, just action as the five massive heavily armored men began to swing their swords into Sherriff Rickert's ground troops. The men had no time to react. Most of the men were unarmed as they milled around the camp. Blood sprayed as throats were slit, limbs dangled as swords crashed through bodies, and screams rang out into the night. Five men rained down hell upon a hundred men in no time at all. A perfect ambush.

A sardonic smile reached the corners of Marcus's mouth as he heard the blood-curdling screams. He looked around the looming cliffs and sniffed the air. It wouldn't be long now. The dragon would come for his woman and he would be waiting for him.

~~~~~

Surprised that they had not been confronted by guards, James and Conall approached the campsite with caution. Their eyes scanned the perimeter, but saw no movement. No soldiers or horses, nothing. They kept their guard up, and continued deeper into the camp. "Something is no right here," James whispered to Conall.

"Aye, do ye smell it?" Conall crinkled up his nose at the foul stench.

"Aye." James knew the stench of death all too well.

They came to a halt, for the sight before them stole their breath. Lifeless bodies littered the ground, and slashed, tattered material from the tents blew into the night breeze like ribbons rippling through the air. Fear of what might have become of Abigale drove James forward. He had to find her, but by the looks of things it seemed unlikely she would have survived the attack.

"There's more here than death, James. It's some kind of magic, I can feel it." Conall bent down and placed his hands on the ground.

A tingling sensation pricked up his spine as his dragon stirred. No doubt he felt it and so did his dragon. "Creepers," James snarled.

"Aye, Death Dragons." Conall stood and wiped his hands on his plaid. "But the question is why are they here?"

"Dinnae know but it can no be good. I can feel it, it's like a pulse of energy running through my blood. I've never felt anything like it." Sweat started to slide down James's face. This feeling left him unnerved.

"I feel it too, my friend."

Every dragon instinct told James to shift, but if there was a chance Abigale was here, James didn't want to scare her.

One tent stood out from the others; it was still intact. James prayed Abigale was in there unharmed and safe. Realization hit him hard in the chest; no one escaped the wrath of the Creepers.

As James approached the tent he saw a head staked outside the entrance. As he got closer he recognized the head. It was the filth who had taken Castle Douglas from him years ago. The filth that James had battled hard against to regain possession. The filth he set on fire and watched burn, so he'd thought. "Rickert," James hissed.

"Looks like he pissed off the wrong person," Conall jested.

James kicked the stake over and entered the tent.

James was not prepared for what he saw. His beautiful Abigale sat hugging her knees inside of an iron-barred birdcage. Abigale looked up and his heart sunk to his stomach. Quickly, she stood.

He pushed his hands through the openings of the cage and cupped Abigale's face. "Are ye hurt, love?"

Dirty tears fell from her deep blue eyes and landed on his hands.

"Hang on. I'll get ye out of there." James kissed her hard. He couldn't believe she was alive. When he broke the kiss, he noticed that her cheek was swollen and there was a cut on her bottom lip. Rubbing his thumb over her lip, he said, "Who hit ye?"

"James, ye must leave now while ye still can," Abigale pleaded. "It's a trap. Marcus, he's going to kill ye."

"Did he do this to ye?"

"Please, James, ye must leave."

"Och lass, do ye have no faith in yer husband? I am a dragon in case ye have forgot."

Abigale didn't take kindly to his jest. "Not even the Black Douglas can survive those… those armored creatures. James, please leave. Save yerself. Marcus won't hurt me, but he will kill ye."

"Abigale, Marcus was the one who tried to kill me. Ye can no trust him for his words are lies."

Conall stood guard just outside the entrance of the tent when the stench of death became stronger and the air surrounding them turned cold. He peeked his head inside the tent. "Ye mind hurrying things up a bit?"

With ease, James pried the iron bars apart just enough for Abigale to step out of the cage. He wrapped his arms tightly around her and whispered in her ear through her auburn hair. "I thought I lost ye, lass."

Abigale held tight around his neck. "I'm no that easy to get rid of."

In no time at all, flaming arrows flew in all directions, piercing the tent and barely missing the three of them. There was no time to hesitate. If they were going to make it out alive, James had to shift. His massive dragon body could shield her from the arrows until she was somewhere safe, but she would have to see him shift. He couldn't do it. He feared she would never be able to look at him in the same light again; the beast inside would be what she remembered, not the man.

James's eyes glowed amber, pupils turned to slits, and fingers turned into talons. "Conall, get Abigale out of here."

Conall knew exactly what was going on; James was about to shift. "Let me shift. Two Dragons are better than one."

"Nay! Get. Her. Out. Of. Here. Now!" James growled the last word.

Enlarged blue eyes stared back at him. Shite, she had seen his talons. "Now, Conall!"

His second in command grabbed Abigale's hand and took off towards the forest, dodging arrows on the way.

The look on Abigale's face told James that he had made the right decision. No way was she ready to see him shift. If he had any say-so about it, she would never see him in dragon form. His dragon was pure evil and menacing. To make things more complicated, he barely had control of it. A young dragon is unpredictable.

Flesh began to peel away, leaving black shimmering scales; his bones began to crack. His spine popped vertebra by vertebra as his human body extended into a massive black dragon with twin horns on top of his head. Leathery black wings unfolded where shoulder blades used to be. In one fluid motion, a wing swept the area, sending the tent flying into the sky.

Like a rain storm, red flames flew through the blackness of the night and showered down pelting James like hail. Arrows struck James in every direction. An earth-rattling roar echoed through the campsite, shaking the tree branches. Wide wings shielded his body from the arrows that threatened to embed in his back. Hopefully Conall could get Abigale to safety; after all he didn't know how long he could distract the archers. He would take as many arrows as necessary in order to keep Abigale alive.

The assault stopped abruptly. Thank the Gods for Magnus and Rory. They had done their job and stopped the archers.

Out of the corner of James's eye he saw Marcus crouching down approaching cautiously with his broadsword drawn, waiting to make his deadly blow. James turned his enormous body toward the bastard and growled low and deep. Nostrils flared, amber eyes glowed as James held Marcus's stare.

"Ye found me, cousin. Took ye long enough," Marcus taunted, wanting James to lose control and make the first mistake. An unpredictable, out of control dragon was a dead one.

Unfolding his wings, James swept the ground, sending blood-drenched dirt into Marcus's face. Frantically he wiped his face. But before James could make contact, Marcus heaved his sword above his head and slammed the metal into James's long neck.

James roared in pain and stumbled back from the deadly blow. Marcus used this to his advantage and quickly approached James, intending to give the final blow. All he had to do was hit the same spot with more force and the beast's head would be hanging on his wall like a prized trophy.

Cocky and confident, Marcus advanced on James, but failed to see a long, black tail sweep across the ground knocking him on his arse. James stood over Marcus before he could catch his breath and get to his feet.

One giant paw grabbed the betrayer's neck, talons pinned his neck to the ground like a cage. James lowered his head just inches from Marcus's. Blood from his wound dripped down his neck and splattered upon

Marcus's face. Hot breath invaded his face as James stared and snarled at him.

Sinister laughter ripped through Marcus. "Cousin, it really doesn't matter who dies here tonight as long as it's a dragon who dies." At that moment Marcus's eyes glowed ice blue with reptilian slits.

Even though James was in dragon form he still had human thoughts inside. Marcus a dragon? Nay, after all these years he would have felt it. Lips peeled back to form a snarl. Not only had Marcus betrayed him; he'd betrayed his Dragonkine brothers. Rage and anger took over reason as he thought of how Marcus had used Abigale and put her in great danger.

"Go ahead, do it, kill me!" Marcus shouted.

~~~~~

Magnus and Rory quickly shifted back into human form after the last archer met his death by dragon. Magnus stopped and observed his surroundings as he felt a prickle of magic slip up his spine. They were closer now to the campsite than before and the stench of death was faint, but enough to tell Magnus that there was much more to this situation then a rescue mission.

"Nay," Magnus grumbled. "I can't believe I didnae recognize it sooner."

Rory walked up to Magnus, tucking his tunic into his plaid. "Recognize what?"

Magnus bent down and grabbed a handful of dry earth. "Blood shall awaken the spirits. The king will rise again."

"Magnus man, ye must stop sputtering in rhymes and riddles. I dinnae understand."

"Rory, we are on the sacred ground of the ancients. We must hurry. Dragon blood can no be spilled on holy ground."

A shrill whistle from Magnus called out to their horses. Two warhorses came charging to their masters from the forest. Without hesitation, Magnus grabbed a lock of mane, threw his muscled leg over the horse, and took the reins in his hands. His horse pranced in anticipation, eager to run. "We must make haste. I'll explain everything soon, but we must stop those fools from killing each other."

Rory shrugged his shoulders and quickly mounted his horse.

~~~~~

James began to crush Marcus's neck until Magnus and Rory ran toward them. "James, ye can no kill him! No here," Magnus yelled. "Ye dinnae understand, if ye kill him Scotland will be destroyed. We will all die."

James turned his head to look at Magnus as if he didn't understand what the daft man was saying.

"Let him go, lad. No blood can be spilled." Magnus challenged James with glowing green eyes. The firmness of Magnus's voice held true; James didn't want to fight an elder, but Marcus had put his lady in harm's way. No way was Marcus leaving this place in one piece, he needed to be punished. One way or the other, a part of the bastard was going to die. He wouldn't shed his blood here tonight but he could take his dragon, leaving him a mortal human. Which he deserved for betraying him.

Without hesitation, James took his free hand and buried it deep into Marcus's chest. Marcus's eyes flew wide open, and he tried desperately to squirm away.

Desperate, Marcus fought to break free, but it was too late; James retrieved his fist from Marcus's chest and with it his beating dragon heart. Marcus screamed in defeat.

201

James released his talons and backed away. No dragon ever enjoyed seeing a Dragonkine's essence destroyed. Every Dragonkine warrior standing by could feel Marcus's loss.

Marcus stood and gripped his chest. "Ye have always thought ye were better than everyone else haven't ye? He spat at James's feet. "Ye take what ye want and do no care about anyone but yerself."

James stood, nostrils flared as he fought back the urge to singe him to ash.

Magnus's voice broke their stare down. "Marcus, ye need to leave well enough alone. Ye are now banished from Scotland. If we see ye here, we will stop at nothing to hunt ye down and kill ye," Magnus stated grimly.

~~~~~

Marcus looked around the campsite. There was no signs of the Creepers anywhere. Strange, he thought, why didn't they help him now? Together, they could slaughter these dragons and fulfill his destiny. Where were they?

"Exiled?" He spat. Being as he'd felt like Scotland had never really opened her arms to him nor his Dragonkine brethren, he laughed. After years of feeling like a failure, he'd cloaked himself as human thinking mayhap he could find acceptance as one. But history could not be erased; he could never forget what the humans had done to his king. In truth, it was because of these vile humans that his life had never been lived to its fullest potential. And wasn't it ironic how his own people called him the traitor, when in fact it was the humans that had betrayed Dragonkine.

The Earth had shifted now, he could feel it. He would right the wrong and soon, verra soon, his kingdom would rise again.

Showing the Dragonkine no signs of weakness, even though he felt every last drop of energy slowly fading, Marcus climbed up on his horse and clucked him into a run as he fled the site.

The path he chose to take took him high into the cold snow-covered mountains deep in the Highlands. No one would venture up there, nor would the bite of the frigid weather chill his bones; ice now replaced his warm blood.

Strength was fading fast and he began to feel faint. He released his hands from his chest. To his surprise, his hand was covered in blood. *Blood?* he thought. When James had taken his dragon heart there was no blood that he'd noticed, but as he looked down into the white snow, a trail of crimson followed him.

His body went limp, causing him to fall off his mount and into a cushion of powdery snow. As he lay there looking up into the sky, flurries covered his face. *Blood has been shed, now hasn't it?* Marcus grinned in triumph as his world slowly filled with darkness. Perhaps enough blood had been shed.

Chapter 23

Danger and delight grow on one stalk. ~ *Scottish Proverb*

"Let me go, Conall. I must see him." Abigale squirmed in Conall's arms.

"Nay, my lady. James does no want you to see him like this."

"I can no stay hidden while Marcus and those creatures kill James. Dragon or not, I must stop him. He will listen to me."

"I'm afraid I can no let you." Conall struggled to gain control of the feisty lass. "Settle down or I'll have to tie ye to a tree."

Finally Abigale came to her senses and settled, for she was no match for the six-foot-five, hulking warrior.

Conall released her. "See, much better. Promise ye'll stay put?"

"Aye." Abigale humphed and paced a short distance, thinking of a way to get past Conall. They were only a few feet away, she could run back to James before he caught her. At least she hoped she could.

"I'll be right back." Conall walked behind a thicket of shrubs.

When it dawned on her what he was doing, she saw the perfect opportunity to run while Conall hid behind the shrubs to relieve himself. Well... aye, she did promise to stay put, but James needed her. Surely, Conall would find it in his heart to forgive a little trickery. She uncrossed her fingers and took off toward the campsite.

Conall walked back to the spot where he'd left Abigale. He was busy looking down at his trews as he finished tying them and said, "James will be fine." When no one answered him, he looked up. "Bloody hell!" She was gone. Quickly, Conall took off after Abigale. Since he knew exactly where she was going, it wouldn't take long to find her. He had to catch her before she reached James.

As Abigale arrived at the camp, Conall caught up to her and grabbed her arm, stopping her from going to James. The commotion attracted the massive black dragon's attention. A deep throaty growl came from the dragon and Conall released her. Relief that James was alive overshadowed her fear and she slowly approached the big beast.

As Abigale got closer, she fought back the urge to run. Never had she seen a dragon before and quite frankly it scared her to death. Pure, raw power radiated off him and the mere size of the beast would cause anyone's heart to stop. Now she understood why James wanted to shelter her from this side of him. Still, inside that dragon lived the man she loved.

Hot air puffed out of the dragon's nostrils as if to calm his nerves. With his head lowered, he gently stepped toward her.

When the dragon was within reaching distance, Abigale placed her shaking hand on its soft velvety nose. Funny, she thought it would be rough. Gaining more confidence, she trailed her hand over his jawline and was amazed how gentle this beast was. She turned her auburn head from side to side, admiring how beautiful this creature was.

The dragon nudged his head gently up against Abigale's chest craving more of her touch. Indeed he did, for she swore she heard him purr when she ran her fingers down his neck. He wrapped his tail around Abigale's waist and pulled her closer. She smiled; she knew this dragon was harmless, after all it was James that watched her when she looked in his swirling amber eyes.

A clap of thunder shook the earth, breaking their embrace. Misty rain fell from the heavens and lightning flickered in the distance. Just like a quick reflex, James unfolded one of his massive black wings over

Abigale's head, shielding her from the storm. Startled, more from the loud thunder than from the dragon, she moved closer, tucking herself beside his neck. Droplets of rain beaded against his skin as she watched the water pour off his wings. As terrifying as this beast was; he was gentle as a kitten.

The wind blew and a cold mist of rain pelted her causing her to shiver. Knowing they would have to find shelter soon, she looked up at James to tell him just that, when she noticed blood trickling down his neck from what looked like a deep gash. "Ye're hurt," she said with concern.

Naturally, the surgeon in her took over and she began to examine the severity of the cut. She ran her fingers around the wound then, as though she thought herself daft, she heard James's voice vibrating through her head. "I'm alright, my *bel ange.*" A shudder rippled through her. She could hear him, yet his lips didn't move. It was as though he was inside of her, talking. Puzzled she took a step back and said, "I can hear ye in my thoughts."

"Aye, through mind speak," James said.

"Mind speak?" Now Abigale knew she must have bumped her head.

"Aye, it's through our bond that ye can hear me."

"Magic," she whispered with amazement. "Aye, some kind of magic."

James began to growl when Magnus approached them. Even though he treaded softly, dragons were extremely possessive of their mates and would not hesitate to kill another if they appeared to be a threat. "James, no need to fash yerself but we need to get the lady oot of the rain before she catches her death." With ease, James lowered his head and gave Abigale a nudge toward Magnus. "He's right. Go with Magnus and I'll be right behind ye."

"My lady, Rory has found us shelter from the rain. Come now we must go. James will follow shortly." Magnus said.

Abigale took one last look at her dragon and then followed Magnus to shelter.

~~~~~

Magnus and Rory stood guard near the entrance of the cave, giving Abigale privacy to shed her wet clothes. She wrapped herself up in a plaid and was now spreading her wet garments over a boulder near the fire Conall had built for her. As he tended to the fire, he didn't look happy with her, for she had lied to him. "Forgive me Conall, I—"

"Aye, I would have done much worse if my love was in danger. So no need for forgiveness my lady. James on the other hand, may have an issue with it. He didnae want ye to see his dragon." Conall placed a dry piece of wood on the flames. "Here, sit down and warm yerself. James will be here soon."

"Thank ye Conall. I can see why James trusts ye. Ye're a good man." Abigale smiled and took a seat next to the fire.

Conall nodded and joined his fellow Dragonkine.

As the fire warmed her cold body, she felt guilty that Magnus, Rory and Conall were still wet and cold. "There's plenty of room next to the fire if ye care to join me." Abigale called out.

"Nay my lady. James would rip our eyes out of their sockets if he caught us even looking at ye with no clothes on," Rory replied over his shoulder.

"Don't be silly. I'm wrapped up."

"Nay lass, trust me. We're just fine," Magnus reassured her.

It seemed like a fortnight had passed, as she waited for James. She missed him and was concerned why it was taking him so long to get to the cave. Had those creatures returned after they left? God, she prayed not. Maybe he wasn't coming back at all. *Nay, he'll be here soon,* she kept telling herself while she raked her fingers through her hair. Before long, she vowed if he didn't show up soon, she would go out looking for him herself.

~~~~~

At that time a very naked and wet James strode into the cave, his eyes intently searching for Abigale. He saw her drying her hair by the fire, wrapped up in a plaid. His heart seized as the flames from the fire flickered across her bare shoulder, making her the most beautiful woman he had ever seen. His cock hardened knowing she was naked as a newborn bairn under that plaid. As their eyes met she smiled and that was his undoing.

James strode over to her with purpose and one purpose only; claiming his woman here and now. He'd been warned long ago, that when mated Dragonkine shifted back to human form, an animalistic urge to claim their woman would consume their every thought. That was exactly what he was experiencing now.

Abigale rose to her feet, but before she could say a word, James fisted the plaid and pulled her close claiming her lips. His hands frantically touched every inch of her body, yet he yearned for more. He broke their kiss long enough to explain. "Sorry love, I need to be inside ye right now."

With a sly grin, Abigale took a step back and dropped the plaid, leaving nothing between them, but hot skin on skin. Pressing their bodies together, he plunged his hands into her damp hair and captured her neck mercilessly with searing kisses and nibbles. Abigale leaned her head back, giving him full access to her; meanwhile her hands roamed his body.

James picked her up so that she straddled him. As soon as his cock brushed against her sex he growled and pushed her up against the cold cave wall. By the saints, he could barely contain himself. The urge grew stronger, pumping through his veins. Abigale's sweet moans wrecked his self-control, the little he had left, and with one hard thrust James entered her.

Abigale's body tensed as she inhaled.

"Did I hurt ye? I'm sorry, love but I can't control it," he panted.

Abigale shook her head no. "Dinnae stop."

James buried his face in her hair, rocked his hips forward and took her fast. He pumped into her with force. She matched every thrust he gave her until he could feel her walls tightening around his shaft. The sweet sting of her nails dug into his back and set him a blaze. "Och lass, what ye do to me." James pumped faster bringing them both over the edge and into sweet orgasmic bliss.

Sweat slid from their bodies as they stayed propped against the wall of the cave. James's legs threatened to shake and give out, but there was no way he was letting her go… not yet. Hell if it was up to him they would stay like this forever. Nothing came close to the feeling of being deep inside her. He thought this is what Heaven must feel like. He was ready to take her again just thinking about it.

He felt Abigale shiver. "Ye're cold. Let's move closer to the fire."

She cupped his face and smiled. "Nay, I'm not cold." Looking down between them she could feel how much he wanted her. She arched a brow and looked back at him. "So soon?"

James smirked. "Well, there are some advantages in being a dragon."

"That so?"

James moved them next to the fire and laid her down on a plaid. He positioned himself between her legs and covered her body with his. "I can go as long as ye need me to." He brushed his fingers through her auburn hair. He gazed from her hair to her deep blue eyes and knew questions were brewing in that pretty head of hers.

Abigale blushed at the thought, then suddenly got serious. "What happened to Marcus?"

He knew she would want to know what had happened and she deserved to know, but to what extent? "Abigale, let it be." Dread filled him when he thought of what he'd done. Destroying a Dragonkine's dragon was not to be taken lightly. James and the other Dragonkine would feel the loss of Marcus for some time to come.

"It's just... oh James, that man killed Marcus's sister."

"She's dead? Ye know this how?"

"Marcus told me. James, he was blackmailed. It seems to me that the man at the campsite, the one who was in charge, had promised Marcus that he would bring his sister back to him if Marcus lured ye to him. That's why Marcus did what he did. He was trying to save his sister."

"The poor lass. I didnae know his sister well. That's a shame. But Marcus should have let me know about his situation. I could have helped, but he chose to betray me instead. He didnae need to keep secrets."

"That's just it, my love, he blames ye for all his misfortune."

"James rolled off Abigale and lay on his back. "Me?"

"Aye, that man wanted his revenge on ye for the brutal way ye killed his men." Abigale shrugged her shoulders. "Well, that's what Marcus believes."

"Since he was in such a truthful mood did he tell ye he too is…" James corrected himself, "was a dragon?"

Her eyes widened, "A dragon?"

"Aye."

Silence fell between them for a while as James decided just how much to tell her when he didn't have all the answers himself. Once back at the castle he'd call counsel and try to figure things out, but now too many questions lay unanswered.

"So, what happened to him?" Abigale fiddled with a strand of James's hair as if she dreaded his answer.

Aye, the question he didn't want to answer. Self-doubt began to gnaw at his gut. Perhaps he'd acted too hastily. In a way he did mourn for him. If he had known beforehand that his sister was dead, most certainly he would have shown mercy. "Abigale it's best no to know all the details. I didnae kill him, but he has been exiled from Scotland."

Abigale closed her eyes and sighed in relief.

"Our world is complicated and it seems it just got more so. I do no have all the answers ye seek. But I can tell ye this, Abigale Bruce, I love ye and I will be the husband ye deserve. I will give ye all the wee bairns yer heart desires. I will give ye the family ye have always wanted. Will ye stay with me, lass?"

Abigale opened her eyes in surprise.

"Och lass, ye dinnae have to look like a deer about to meet an arrow."

A giggle escaped her mouth and a tear threatened to fall. "I love ye too James Douglas… even the Black Douglas." No longer holding back her excitement, she threw herself on top of him and kissed him deeply.

Everything James could ever want in his life was right here in his arms and he silently vowed that he would spend every moment showing his *bel ange* from the loch just how much he loved her.

~~~~~

After Abigale fell asleep, James donned his trews and walked out toward the entrance of the cave. The rain had finally stopped. Rory and Conall were propped up against the cave's wall sleeping as Magnus stood watch.

The whole situation with Marcus kept replaying in his mind. Furthermore, Magnus's words had made no sense to him. Not spilling blood and Scotland being destroyed continued to be a puzzle to him and the only way to solve it was to speak with Magnus.

Magnus was sitting down leaning up against the cave's outside walls with his long legs stretched out in front of him. "I thought ye might come looking for me, lad."

James crossed his arms over his chest. "Did ye know?"

Magnus stared off into the distance. "Nay. I can no explain that one, my friend. 'Tis no an easy task to cloak one's dragon, especially in the company of other dragons."

Thank the Gods Magnus didn't know. One man's betrayal had been enough to swallow; he couldn't bear to believe Magnus would betray him as well. "I think I might have over reacted, I should no have taken his dragon. He told Abigale that his sister is dead and he blames me for it. In fact he blames me for all his misfortunes. That's why he took Abigale from me. He knew I would come for her then he could hand me over to Rickert."

Magnus was stunned. "I can no trust my ears lad, the Black Douglas has a conscience?"

Aggravated, James shifted his weight on his heels and shot Magnus a scowl.

Magnus smiled at the distress. "Every old bone in my body tells me that Marcus had the plan all along. Aye, Rickert was blackmailing him but Marcus knew where the holy ground lay buried. Why else would he have tried to kill ye, here? The lad is up to something wicked."

"Holy ground?"

"Ye felt it, the magic?" Magnus said.

"Aye, both me and Conall."

"I wish I had recognized this place sooner. I had hoped to have never come back here."

"What do ye mean?"

"This is our kingdom." Magnus tapped his hand on the ground beside him. "This is where it all began and ended for Dragonkine. Our king waits to be awoken."

James couldn't believe what he was hearing. Underneath them lay their long lost kingdom. A kingdom he had only heard of, yet he knew he followed a long line of warrior ancestors.

Magnus continued. "Dragon blood can no be spilled on holy ground, it will awaken the seven and our king. And if our king rises," Magnus shook his head, "his vengeance will rain down upon every human. I can feel it, James. If ye love yer wife, we must no let this happen."

Now what Marcus had done was all making sense to him. James began to pace with his hands on his hips. "So killing me here... tonight... would have awakened our king. But why? Why would he want the king to return?"

"I wish I knew." Magnus grew dark like a cloud ready to storm.

"When Conall and I were in Rickert's campsite we felt and smelled the death dragons –"

"Death dragons?" With alarm Magnus jumped to his feet. "'Tis no good, no good at all. Are ye sure, lad?"

"Aye, there's no mistaking that stench nor the destruction they left behind. At least one hundred men slaughtered and Rickert's head on a spike."

Magnus whistled for his horse. "I must leave."

"Magnus, what's going on here?" Something had to be terribly wrong for Magnus to leave suddenly. This left James unnerved.

"I must talk with the elders immediately. If the death dragons didnae kill Marcus, we might well have a bigger problem on our hands then we think." Magnus hopped up on his mount and reined in the feisty steed. "In the meantime I think ye've done enough damage to Marcus that he won't be a threat for a while, but hear my words, lad, don't take yer eyes far from him. Keep yer lass safe until I return." With nothing more said Magnus took off deep into the glen, racing with God speed.

James was left dumbfounded. Aye some questions he sought after were clear, but now a whole new puzzle piece had been found.

Epilogue

Abigale was cleaning up after seeing her last patient of the day. Her little stone dwelling with a thatched roof was easily accessible located in the clan's village. Nicely placed along the east side, the bright morn sun gave it a welcoming feeling. At first, James wasn't keen on the idea of his wife and the lady of the castle working and furthermore being away from the protection of Black Stone on the Hill.

"Idle hands are the Devil's tools," she'd told her husband.

"Och lass, yer hands dinnae need to stay idle." He'd wriggled his brows. "Ye can do the Devil's work on my body any time ye want."

She remembered that sly sexy grin of his and smiled as she tucked the corner of the sheet under the cot's mattress.

But the point was made, even though he tried to distract her; clan Douglas needed a good surgeon/healer and she was the best.

In time, James granted her her own place to practice, but there was no debating about the guards who would stay outside her hut, another ten that patrolled the village and the five placed next door at the cordwainer. Once Mac, the shoemaker, found out who was next door to him, he made sure to deliver a pair of beautiful shoes for Abigale and the girls at least once a month. He claimed that a beautiful woman should have beautiful shoes.

As Abigale finished putting clean sheets on one of the cots, her assistant pulled the linen sheet curtain back that partitioned the room off from two other rooms and announced, "My lady, I've cleaned the other two rooms and rinsed out the wash basins. Is there more ye would like me to do?"

"Nay, Anna. I thank ye kindly for yer help today." Abigale stood and placed her hands on her swollen belly. "I dunno what I'd do without ye." She smiled.

"How much longer until the wee one arrives?" Anna reached over and touched Abigale's belly.

Abigale didn't mind the occasional belly rub. In fact it reminded her of how much she loved the wee one already.

"Oh Anna, I hope soon. The babe must be a boy, for his kicks are strong." Abigale laughed.

"Shall I wait until ye're done? I'm in no hurry."

Abigale walked past Anna out into an open area where she could look out a small window. Shelves of glass containers filled with herbs and concoctions framed the window. Adjusting one of the jars, Abigale looked out the window and saw James approaching the village. A brilliant smile spread across her face and instantly her hands began to rub her belly again. "Nay Anna, go home to yer family and I'll see ye in the morn."

"Fare well this eve, my lady." Anna picked up the basket of fruit Abigale had brought her this morn and quit the room.

Observing the space around her, Abigale couldn't be happier; she was living her dream. A blessing indeed, James had allowed her to practice her skills and live out her passion. But most of all, she had her independence. Most women didn't have that freedom. As she'd had her freedom taken from her back at the abbey, Abigale vowed she would assist any woman seeking their independence. Anna had come to her not so long ago, badly beaten. Her husband, a drunk, had beat her. After Abigale told James about Anna's situation, Anna was under the protection of clan Douglas and as for the drunken husband… he was never heard of again.

Oh if Sister Kate could see me now, she thought. Abigale looked down at her belly. Aye, if she could see her now.

Breaking her reminiscing, James opened the door to her hut and two beautiful girls charged in before he could step over the threshold. The girls, with their blonde hair bouncing, greeted Abigale with hugs and kisses. "Oh my loves, I've missed ye too." Abigale embraced the girls. Peering up from their embrace Abigale locked eyes with her husband's swirling amber depths and those fiery butterflies returned.

James entered the room and made his way to Abigale. He placed his hands on her belly and kissed her deeply. "I've missed ye two today."

"Aye, we've missed ye too, my love."

"Are ye ready for some fresh air, *bel ange?* I thought we would sit by the old rowan tree and let the girls play for a while. What say ye?"

"I think 'tis a beautiful idea." Abigale smiled up at James and kissed him.

"Good." James motioned for them to step outside.

Indeed it was a gorgeous day. For once there was no threat of rain. Once outside the girls raced to their favorite spot and started to pick wild flowers.

Abigale and James walked beside his mare when Abigale noticed something strange. "James, how much is the lad at the stable feeding yer horse?"

James looked at Abigale as if she had grown two heads. "Why ye ask?"

"She's fat."

"Fat? Nay."

Abigale stopped and James followed. She walked in front of the horse, rubbing the mare's nose. "Shh lassie." Continuing around to the horse's side, she ran her hand over its belly. "James, is there a possibility she could be pregnant?"

Still looking confused, he joined Abigale and did his own examination of the mare's swollen belly. "Fergus, ye sly dog."

Abigale faced James. "What do ye mean?"

"Do ye remember the night when I brought ye back to bed from sleeping in the stall with Fergus?"

"Aye."

"Well, let's just say I rewarded him for good behavior." James winked.

Abigale slapped his chest. "Ye mean to tell me Shadow is now pregnant with Fergus's baby?"

"Looks like it, love."

Abigale's laughter soon turned to tears.

"What's wrong? Did I—"

"Oh nay, James, these are happy tears." Standing on the tips of her toes, she hugged her husband. Now a part of her trusted friend would live on.

They broke their embrace and made it over to the rowan tree. James spread out a plaid then helped Abigale to sit. Next he handed her a basket of fruit and bread and teased Abigale with one of Alice's famous oatcakes.

Finally as James made his way to the blanket, the ground below began to tremble. He paused for a moment and looked down at the earth.

"What's wrong, James." Abigale was beginning to feel alarmed when he didn't respond right away. "James?"

As quickly as the earth shook, it stopped. Not wanting to frighten Abigale, James shrugged the rumble off but deep down his worse fears were beginning to surface.

"'Tis nothing. We're fine."

"James, I felt it too. Ye can no tell me that was nothing."

He leaned his back against the tree as he joined Abigale on the blanket and motioned for her to come sit with him. "Dinnae worry, it's no good for the babe." He smiled.

Abigale quickly forgot about the disturbance as she found herself wrapped up in his loving embrace. Her back pressed up against his chest all the while James kissed her neck and rubbed her belly. How could she be so lucky to have a man who loved her so much? Truly she felt like her life was complete.

"I have something for ye," James whispered in her ear. "Close yer eyes."

She did exactly what she was told. She could hear James rustling around in his satchel next to him.

"Open yer eyes."

What she saw took her breath away. An elegant silver torc with dragon heads on each of the ends stared back at her. The dragon's eyes were made out of amber. The torc shined as the sun's rays hit the metallic necklace making it sparkle. It was fit for a queen.

"Oh James, this is —"she was at a loss for words; the piece was beyond any riches she had ever seen.

"Here, let me see how it looks on ye." James pushed Abigale's hair over her shoulder and placed the torc around her neck.

Touching the fine piece, she turned to face him. "It fits perfectly." She placed her hand on his cheek and kissed him.

"Abigale Bruce, I love ye. Hell, I loved ye from the moment I saw ye that morn at the loch. I'm honored to be yer husband and I'm most definitely honored that ye will be the mother of my children. I hope that ye can learn to love my dragon just as much as I love ye."

Tears were building up again. She was truly loved and she loved every bit of this man sitting in front of her, even the dragon. "I love all of ye and I could no be any happier than ye've made me." Tears broke through and slid down her cheeks.

James took her face in his hands and wiped away the wetness from her cheeks with his thumbs. "Happy tears?"

"Aye, happy tears." Abigale smiled.

Glossary

Bairn - Baby or small child

Bele ange - French for beautiful angel

Bonny - Beautiful

Byre - Cow shed

Chemise/Shift - A piece of clothing that looks like a light, loose dress and that is worn by women as underwear or in bed

Circator - Monks/Nuns who ensure that all Monks/Nuns were obeying abbey rules.

Cannae - can not

Cordwainer - Shoemaker

Daft - Silly

Dinnae - Don't

Didnae - Didn't

Dunderhead - Silly

Hogget - A sheep up to the age of one year that has yet to be sheared

Knight Banneret - A medieval knight who could command men in battle under his own banner

Pas aussi belle que vous - French for "Not as beautiful as you"

Sassenach - Derogatory an English person

About the Author

Victoria Zak lives in the sunshine state with her husband, two beautiful children, and three furry friends. Before having kids, Victoria spent fifteen years in the veterinary business and volunteered in pet rescue.

"One of my most rewarding jobs was finding unwanted animals their forever homes."

A writing career was the last item listed on her bucket list, until she discovered that she wanted to put her stories on paper and breathe life into her characters. Her love for Scotland, curiosity of history, and passion for romance has inspired her to write her first book, Highland Burn.

"Fourteenth century Scotland was a fascinating time in history. Not only was Scotland fighting for their freedom from the English king, their own people fought each other; clan vs clan. Though being a woman of the twenty-first century, I wouldn't want to live in those unsettled times. But writing historical fiction paranormal romance allows me to escape into their world and breathe a fresh air of romance and magic into that era, which I love to do."

Victoria loves to hear from her readers. You can connect with her through her Amazon author page, Facebook, Twitter @VictoriaZak2, G+, and her website www.victoriazakromance.com.

26132792R00138

Made in the USA
San Bernardino, CA
19 November 2015